Best Practices of Spell Design

A COMPUTATIONAL FAIRY TALE

The *Computational Fairy Tales* Series:

Computational Fairy Tales

Best Practices of Spell Design

Best Practices of Spell Design

A Computational Fairy Tale

Jeremy Kubica

Cover design and art by Meagan O'Brien
Interior design by Marjorie Carlson
Set in Bell MT, Courier New, Gill Sans, and WWDesigns

To Regan

Contents

Preface

THIS BOOK IS ABOUT the best practices of writing software. It covers the practical aspects that are often learned or reinforced through experience, such as the value of testing and the importance of comments. It introduces the concepts that are vital to writing code that can be maintained by others.

This book is not a comprehensive text, but rather a high-level introduction. The goal is to introduce the reader to a variety of good programming practices and encourage the reader to think about how to write readable, well-tested, and maintainable programs. Reading this book alone won't make you a better programmer. Instead, the hope is that it will encourage you to think about your programming practices and what it takes to write better code.

This book assumes some experience with programming, but does not require knowledge of any specific language. The concepts in this book are meant to apply to a range of programming languages and problem domains.

Understanding the Problem

MARCUS, THE MOST POWERFUL wizard in the kingdom, was worried. He brought his face up to the castle wall, peering at each crack. He had never seen damage this bad—at least not from a spell. All bets were off when catapults or wrecking balls were involved.

"You should have called *me*," he admonished.

King Fredrick remained silent, his fists clenched. Beside him, his steward gasped. Only four people in the entire kingdom could snap at the king without punishment. Until now, Marcus had never tested this freedom.

"A terrible mess," said Marcus. "Who did this?"

"The wizard Hannaldous," answered the king's steward.

"A hack!" cried Marcus. "A cheap, ignorant hack! You should have called me."

The steward paused before continuing, his calm expression unwavering.

"Of course, we would have called you had we known of your expertise with this spell," responded the steward. "However, we were unaware of this spell's very existence until our recent audience with Hannaldous. He assured us that this spell was his own unique invention. Had you told us of it earlier, we could have avoided this unpleasantness."

"*Obviously* this spell is his own invention," Marcus said with a sigh. "I've never seen anything like it, myself. Unfortunately, it appears that Hannaldous hadn't exactly perfected it yet," Marcus added with all of the tact he could muster. He resisted the urge to rant about Hannaldous's incompetence. The evidence was already overwhelming.

"Do you know what went wrong?" asked the king, speaking for the first time since Marcus's arrival.

"No," answered Marcus. "But I know what he did wrong."

"I believe that is what the king asked," said the steward. For a brief instant, his calm mask faltered. His tone dropped from polite down to cordial.

"I'm not being clear," Marcus said, waving his arm toward the wall with dramatic flourish. He shifted into the lecturing tone that he used when speaking to a new apprentice or anyone without the faintest knowledge of magic.

"I apologize for my ambiguity," he continued. "Hannaldous's mistake was not understanding the problem. He tried to apply a shield spell to the wall, but something didn't work. He knew what he wanted, but didn't take time to understand the details. He rushed things. That is what *he* did wrong.

"However, I don't know what went wrong with the spell *itself*. I need time to investigate."

"How bad is it?" the king asked.

Marcus paused for a moment while trying to think of an encouraging answer. Nothing came to mind.

"Bad," he answered.

"The castle?" asked the steward, a note of true concern slipping into his voice.

"It's already starting to crumble," Marcus answered. "If we don't reverse the spell soon, it will be lost."

The steward let out a startled squeak. Marcus politely pretended not to notice.

Marcus continued, speaking to the king. "Sir, there is one more thing. If left unchecked, the spell will spread to all structures made of stone or wood. The whole town is in danger—excluding, of course, some of the more artistic structures, like the Ventwick Tower of Mud."

"How long do we have?" asked the king.

"About a month for the castle and a few more for the town,"

answered Marcus.

The king nodded. His face betrayed no emotion. His eyes remained fixed on the wall of the castle. "Can you fix it?"

Marcus looked back at the castle's wall. The botched spell was powerful, and it had a head start of at least two days. A layer of fine dust on the stones indicated their deteriorating condition. "I can try."

"Let us know if you need anything. The resources of the kingdom are at your disposal."

"Can you arrange an audience with Hannaldous?" Marcus asked. "The first step in designing a spell, or counterspell as it may be, is thoroughly understanding the problem. I would very much like to speak to him about this spell so I can understand what needs to be done."

"As would I," the king agreed.

"It appears that Hannaldous left the kingdom," the steward explained. "Shortly after casting the spell, he departed to Venice. He claims to have received an urgent request, although the pigeon master could not find a record of any messages."

Marcus almost laughed. Given the mess Hannaldous had made, Marcus didn't doubt that he had fled. Hannaldous had probably started planning his escape the instant he chanted the last phrase and noticed the stone weakening. If anything, Marcus was surprised that he had stayed around long enough to make up an excuse.

"However, in his rush, the wizard appears to have forgotten to pack. His notebooks were in his room," added the steward.

"I guess that's better than nothing," said Marcus without any enthusiasm. "Please send the notebooks to my laboratory. I shall make this my sole priority."

As Marcus walked away from the castle, he silently bemoaned the task ahead. Hannaldous's spell bore all the signs of a poorly constructed spell. Yet another case of shortcuts and poor spell-writing practices. Now it was up to Marcus to understand it and repair the damage.

The Importance of Good Programming Practices

S HELLY LEANED AGAINST THE bakery's counter. Across from her, Ivan was scooping small blobs of blueberry-flecked dough into a muffin tin. Both teens tried to ignore the shouts from the back room.

"I told you a hundred times!" bellowed the voice. "Didn't you listen?"

Shelly's eyes darted toward the door. "What did she do?" she mouthed.

Ivan glanced back. Then, deeming it safe, he leaned in to answer. "Margaret messed up an entire batch of cream puffs." His voice came out below a whisper, barely audible over the hum of the ovens.

"So?" asked Shelly, matching his tone. "It's her first week. She's bound to make a few mistakes. All apprentices do."

Ivan stole another glance at the door before responding, "Not like this and not in Breadista's program. You don't make this kind of mistake after your first day."

"What did she do?" Shelly asked again.

"She mixed up teaspoons and tablespoons," he answered. Shelly could tell from his expression that this represented a grievous error in the bakery.

"She added nine *tablespoons* of salt," Ivan added.

"Oh," started Shelly, trying to force her face to convey the seriousness that the situation appeared to deserve. Against her will, a smile flickered across her face. "That must have been salty," she said.

"It ruined the recipe," Ivan said.

"By making salty cream puffs?" asked Shelly. A small laugh escaped from her mouth before she could stifle it. She coughed, hoping to cover it up.

"In baking, those types of mistakes are serious," said Ivan, who hadn't found the same humor in the situation. "You have to make sure you're using the correct units throughout a recipe. Otherwise, it can be disastrous. You should appreciate that. You need to measure out ingredients for potions, right?"

"Sure," admitted Shelly, thinking back to her own latest failed potion. The parrot had sneezed for two solid hours. "But when I use the wrong units of measurement, something explodes. Margaret made salty cream puffs."

"Baking is serious work," Ivan insisted. "In order to create the finest edible masterpieces, we must adhere to the strictest baking practices, such as careful testing, well-written recipes, and consistent units. I've spent three years learning the trade, and it will be another five before I can open my own shop. It's not a game for those without dedication. It's for true professionals. For masters."

"Otherwise you could end up with salty cream puffs," added Shelly.

"Stop saying 'salty cream puffs' as though it's a real thing," Ivan said. A look of hurt flashed across his face.

"I'm sorry," said Shelly. "I'm just giving you a hard time. Believe me, I understand the importance of good practices in creating spells or recipes. I once translated a potion from Old Britanish, but forgot to change all the units to the Royal Standard. The entire load of laundry came out a deep purple and tried to wiggle away."

Ivan stared at her.

"Anyway, *you* seem to have gotten the hang of it," said Shelly. "Your blueberry muffins are amazing—which reminds me, I promised Veronica that I would get her one."

Ivan visibly cheered at the comment. "There's a batch in the oven now," he said. "They should be ready in about ten minutes. You really like them?"

Shelly nodded enthusiastically.

"Well, Breadista is one of the best teachers in the world. He teaches more than just the recipes. Anyone can teach recipes. Breadista teaches us how to think like bakers."

Ivan's face lit up as he spoke. He became animated, waving at the baskets of bread. A wispy cloud of flour trailed from his arms.

The words continued to tumble out of his mouth with a mixture of pride and pure excitement. "Within the first year, I had to learn muffins, breads, doughnut, and bagels. Over a hundred recipes total. Forty recipes for muffins alone, including the triple bran wheat loaf. I'll admit that it wasn't the most exciting year, but afterward, I felt like I could *create* something. Do you ever feel like that?"

"I'm still on the basic potions," admitted Shelly. "Wizard training requires a lot of foundation."

"That's too bad," said Ivan. "I'm sure you'll get to something interesting soon."

"I've done interesting spells," Shelly said. "Like … I helped Marcus with the Spell of Glowing Ants. You'd be surprised at how much mold we needed to collect for that one."

"You seem to spend a lot of time collecting mold," Ivan said thoughtfully. "But I meant doing a whole spell by yourself. Creating something new. That's the goal, right? It would be awful to spend the rest of your career collecting mold for someone else's potions like a professional mold scraper. My third cousin Jimmy is a scraper, and he hates it.

"Don't worry, though. I hear that most wizards' apprentices don't get to do anything interesting for a long time. Some never do. It's not like baking."

He smiled reassuringly.

Shelly forced a smile in return.

"Want to see my latest project?" asked Ivan after a moment. "I'm working on an eight-layer wedding cake."

"Eight layers?" asked Shelly.

"Yeah," said Ivan. "It's going to be great. It's going to be the culmination of this year's work. I had to learn a bunch of new cake-decorating practices, like separating the repeated steps for making candy flowers into its own task."

Shelly looked back at him with a blank expression.

"Like a subrecipe," explained Ivan. "A set of steps that you use over and over in different contexts."

"Sure," Shelly muttered.

"Anyway," continued Ivan, "Breadista is the best teacher in the world. He introduces us to concepts that would have taken years of painful trial and error to master."

"I'm sure he's wonderful," said Shelly.

"He pushes his apprentices to *create*," added Ivan with flowing enthusiasm. "He says that creating new works of art is the way toward mastery."

"Uh-huh," said Shelly. "Good for him … and you."

"And, of course, he never makes me collect mold," Ivan joked.

Shelly grunted a laugh and developed a sudden interest in the countertop.

"Want to see the cake?" asked Ivan.

"Why not?" Shelly said.

"Okay," said Ivan. "Just one minute. I just need to get this batch of nut oat muffins finished first."

Shelly slumped further against the counter. She watched him prepare the mixture, humming to himself the whole time. Then, Shelly noticed the bowl of chopped nuts.

Does the process really matter? she thought to herself. *How bad can a muffin mistake be?*

Readable Code

"A DISGRACE!" SAID MARCUS. HE threw his feather quill to the table.

His apprentice Shelly looked up from her own scroll. Panic flooded her mind as she tried to place the context. She stifled the unbearable thought that he had learned about the earlier incident at the bakery. She reassured herself that he was probably referring to her work, although that wasn't much of an improvement.

"This spell is an abomination," Marcus complained.

Shelly wondered which of her recent assignments he was reading and what she had done wrong. She stole a glance at the scroll.

Marcus saw her.

"Come look at this," he instructed. "It's the world's finest example of how not to write a spell. Two hundred and fifty-six pages of terribly constructed instructions. And, as far as I can tell, absolutely none of it was properly thought out! It's a wonder Hannaldous hasn't accidentally turned himself into a Macedonian river slug yet. At least that would improve his intelligence."

Shelly placed her own quill on the table and walked over to view the offending scroll. The spell bore no resemblance to anything she had seen before. A tangled mass of scrawled instructions occupied the entire page. Words were packed tight without any spaces, as if in an attempt to conserve every last bit of parchment. At one point an *i,* a *t,* and an *o* from different lines all overlapped. The resulting mess reminded Shelly more of pictograms than of text.

"What does it do?" asked Shelly.

"I'm not sure yet," answered Marcus. "It was intended to provide a shield to the castle walls. Unfortunately, the author is an idiot. As a result, the walls are now crumbling."

"That isn't good."

"No. It isn't," agreed Marcus. "Now *I* have to read through this mess and undo the damage."

Then, turning to Shelly, Marcus adopted his teaching tone. "What problems do you see with this spell?"

"Well …" Shelly stalled as she studied the scroll. "It doesn't have any empty space, the handwriting is terrible, the potions' names are incomprehensible, the variable names are too similar, it doesn't have any structure, and I think the author spilled at least three cups of coffee on it."

Marcus nodded his approval. "In other words, it isn't readable."

"Not to me," Shelly agreed. "But maybe Hannaldous preferred to record his spells this way."

"Ha!" cried Marcus. "This is a classic example of a poorly written spell. It's nearly impossible to understand or maintain. Why do I insist that your spells be readable?"

"So you can check them?" ventured Shelly.

"I insist on readable spells so *any* wizard can read, understand, and modify them! Recording spells is vital for passing along knowledge, but it's more than that. In order to use or modify someone else's spell, you have to be able to understand it."

"Isn't that the same as making them readable for you?" Shelly asked. "No one else is going to read my assignments."

"More importantly, you need to be able to read your *own* spells," Marcus replied. "I know you think that because you created the spell, you'll never forget it. Ha! You're lying to yourself. Give it a year or two and you'll have no idea what the spell means. Once you reach my age, you only need to wait about thirteen minutes to forget the details. Readability isn't just about other wizards."

"What about this spell?" asked Shelly. "Obviously, Hannaldous cast it."

"Yes," agreed Marcus. "He cast the spell, and he got it wrong.

Messed things up royally, too. I would bet Hannaldous got all tangled up while trying to follow his own spell."

Marcus threw his arms up in frustration as he worked himself into a full, though admittedly enjoyable, tirade. "How can you assemble a spell this complex without being able to understand what you did five pages ago? It's a perfect recipe for mistakes. Mistakes skulk around in the clutter, like mold spores in a bread cabinet. They lurk about, waiting to turn a reasonable attempt at spell design into a fuzzy green dinner roll."

"Maybe he was in a hurry," offered Shelly.

"That's no excuse," said Marcus. "When was the last time you saw an architect scrawl out blueprints for a castle with a purple crayon because she was in a hurry? Never! To be useful, spells and blueprints must both be understandable."

"And dinner rolls should never be green or fuzzy?" added Shelly, trying to follow along.

"I expect every spell you write to maintain the highest readability standards," Marcus added, ignoring her last comment. He paused, watching her for a sign of acknowledgment.

Shelly nodded.

Marcus turned back to the scroll and sighed. "I suppose you should get back to your work," he said. "And I should get back to this mess."

For once, Shelly was eager to return to her studies.

Understandable IF Statements

T HE STEWARD LOOKED UP as a junior scribe entered his office. He held up a finger, stopping the scribe on the far side of the room. The steward made a final note on his parchment, moved it to one of the three in-progress piles on his desk, and then motioned the young boy forward.

"I brought a draft for your inspection," the scribe said. He held out a sheet of parchment labeled "Castle Regulations Temporary Amendment 14b: New Conditions for Prolonging Structural Integrity."

The steward had been expecting the document. He took the parchment and read it silently. He nodded a few times.

"All technically correct," said the steward, "But you must clean it up before distributing it to the staff."

The scribe looked shocked. He had been meticulous in his transcription. His perfect block letters would put the other scribes to shame.

"Clean it up, sir? I believe it meets the castle's legibility standard—exceeds it, even. Is there a specific letter that you feel is misshapen? Is it the letter *e*?" Panic seeped into the poor boy's voice as his eyes scanned the parchment. He was fiercely proud of his *e*'s.

The steward glanced back down at the parchment. "No. Your handwriting is flawless, as always. My concern is the construction of the IF statement. These instructions must be easily understood by all the castle's employees, contractors, vendors, and visitors."

"But the conditions are logically exact," argued the scribe.

"Not even a Boolean could find fault in them."

"Booleans are not the target audience," the steward noted. "And, as I have already said, the conditions are valid. I am concerned about the understandability."

The scribed frowned. "Understandability?"

"Allow me to demonstrate," said the steward. He pulled a fresh sheet of parchment from a perfect stack on the bottom left corner of his desk.

"Let us begin with the rules for construction projects," said the steward, pointing to a block of finely printed text.

```
IF ((time < 1 day) OR ((time < 1 week) AND (workers <
  5)) OR ((time < 2 hours) AND (workers < 2))):
  IF ((time < 2 hours) AND (workers < 2)):
    IF (the work needs power tools):
      prohibit the work
    ELSE:
      allow the work
  ELSE:
    IF (the work needs power tools):
      prohibit the work
    ELSE:
      allow the work in 4-hour shifts
ELSE:
  IF (the work needs power tools):
    prohibit work
  ELSE:
    consult with steward
```

"First, the organization of the initial Boolean statement makes it difficult to read. The condition consists of three separate clauses that are ORed together. However, that structure is not at all apparent. It would be clearer if you broke up the lines to match the expressions."

The steward wrote an expression on the blank parchment:

```
IF ((time < 1 day) OR
  (time < 1 week) AND (workers < 5)) OR
  ((time < 2 hours) AND (workers < 2))):
```

"And, in this case, you could further improve the readability by removing the constituent Boolean clauses and capturing them in well-named variables."

```
is_small_job = (time < 2 hours) AND (workers < 2)
is_medium_job = ((time < 1 week) AND (workers < 5))
  OR (time < 1 day)
IF (is_small_job OR is_medium_job):
```

"Next, consider the organization of the rules. Regardless of job size, we prohibit work that requires power tools. You can therefore combine several IF tests by bringing this condition to the top."

```
is_small_job = (time < 2 hours) AND (workers < 2)
is_medium_job = ((time < 1 week) AND (workers < 5))
  OR (time < 1 day)
IF (the work does not need power tools):
  IF (is_small_job):
    allow the work
  ELSE IF (is_medium_job):
    allow the work in 4-hour shifts
  ELSE:
    consult with steward
ELSE:
  prohibit work
```

As he wrote, he added, "I cannot emphasize enough the risk now posed by a simple drill. It is imperative that we adhere to the 'no power tools' condition. These rules must be absolutely clear."

Once the steward finished writing the new conditions, he

looked up. "Have you any questions?"

The scribe studied the parchment for a minute, forcing himself not to comment on the steward's handwriting. The letters were well formed, but too linear and cold. Even the *o*'s didn't seem round enough.

"What I have is correct, though. Isn't it?" asked the scribe.

"It is correct, although it was difficult to confirm that fact," the steward said. "More importantly, it would be difficult for most of the castle vendors to follow it correctly. Remember, readability is not just about handwriting."

He handed both the draft rules and his notes to the scribe.

"Please clean up the conditions and bring the regulations back within the hour," the steward concluded in his usual polite tone. "We have no time to waste in implementing these new policies."

Then he forced a pleasant smile, waved the scribe out, and turned back to his own stacks of paperwork.

Functions

THREE DAYS LATER, SHELLY found Marcus hunched over Hannaldous's scroll. He sat, head in his hands, mumbling to himself. Panic coursed through her. A mumbling wizard was never a good sign.

"Are you okay?" Shelly asked.

Marcus looked up at her, his eyes bloodshot. He had been working on the scroll nonstop but had made little progress.

"Functions," Marcus croaked. Then clearing his throat, "Hundreds of pages of spells with only one function."

"Functions?" asked Shelly. She had heard the term before but hadn't reached it in her own training. She silently cursed Marcus's excruciatingly thorough teaching style.

"Subspells, if you prefer," explained Marcus, "Functions are separate blocks of instructions that can be reused throughout a complex spell. Each function has a single, well-defined goal—one thing that it does. And it has clear inputs and outputs.

"Remember the Spell of Glowing Ants?" asked Marcus. "It had a function called IncreaseLuminosityOfSurface."

He rummaged through a desk drawer until he found the spell.

"Here's the function," he noted, pointing to a section of instructions.

```
IncreaseLuminosityOfSurface(surface):
    make two small wand loops in the air
    point wand at surface
    clearly state "get ye brighter"
    flick wand one time at surface
```

"Admittedly, it's a simple function. But we called it at least a dozen times." He pointed to a few blocks of instructions further down in the spell:

```
FOR each leg:
   IncreaseLuminosityOfSurface(leg)
```

and then, on the next page:

```
WHILE (ant is not bright enough):
   IncreaseLuminosityOfSurface(thorax)
   measure the brightness
```

"It's the same instructions each time, so we can break it out into a function. The only part that changes is the input," said Marcus. "Imagine if we had to write out the instructions separately for each leg and the thorax."

Shelly thought for a while as she studied the spell. "Functions make the spell more compact by removing repeated lines?" she ventured, remembering her recent discussion with Ivan about subrecipes.

"That's one benefit," Marcus agreed. "Functions also make the spell more readable and reduce errors. You improve readability by replacing a chunk of spell with a single, well-named function. You reduce errors by having one implementation, which you can thoroughly test."

Marcus turned back to Hannaldous's scroll and waved around seemingly at random. "Do you see these eight blocks I circled in red?" he asked.

Shelly nodded. The circles were hard to miss; she had been conditioned to notice them. A feeling of angst welled up inside her as she flashed back to her own previous assignments, parchments soggy with red ink. She turned aside, clenching her eyes shut, and took a few deep breaths. "This is not my assignment," she reminded herself in the faintest whisper.

Marcus didn't notice the reaction.

"Eight blocks of instructions doing the exact same thing!" Marcus scoffed. "Each one clears a surface of insects. This one clears the castle rocks. This one clears the ground within an inch of the castle walls. This one clears a sandwich—why would he need that one?" Marcus trailed off with a worried look on his face.

After a moment he shrugged and continued, "Anyway, they all do the same thing. Or, at least, they're supposed to. The one to clear his sandwich has a small mistake and won't work on beetles.

"Imagine how much simpler this scroll would look if Hannaldous had used a function," Marcus continued. "And, if he had tested it, he would have ensured that his sandwich stayed beetle-free."

He copied Hannaldous's instructions into a ClearBugsFromSurface function on a clean piece of parchment.

"After he wrote out the instructions once as a separate function, he could then call ClearBugsFromSurface(walls) to replace these 50 lines on page 63," said Marcus, pointing to the corresponding block of instructions. "And ClearBugsFromSurface(ground) could replace the instructions on pages 103, 105, and 106."

Suddenly the concept clicked into place in Shelly's brain.

"It's like a guitar!" exclaimed Shelly.

"What?" asked Marcus with a look of annoyance. "How is it anything like a guitar?"

"Each chord is a function," explained Shelly, "Any chord, say, B-minor for example, requires the correct finger positions and strum pattern. You need to execute multiple motions, but they're all represented by two letters in the sheet music. You learn a few functions, one for each chord, and apply them repeatedly throughout every song."

"I suppose that's true," agreed Marcus.

"Or cooking," continued Shelly, beaming with excitement. "I bet lots of recipes say 'Make fifty pounds of pastry dough,' but that's just a function. Making dough is a set of instructions it-self. It has input ingredients. You use flour, right? It even has an output.

"Or—"

"Yes, yes," interrupted Marcus. "Functions are everywhere, except in this scroll. If only Hannaldous had possessed your excitement for functions, interpreting this mess would be easier."

As Marcus shifted his attention back to the scroll, Shelly lingered behind him.

"Umm ..." she started.

Marcus looked back up.

"What should I do today?" she asked.

Marcus glanced around the room as though looking for inspiration.

"I suppose today is as good a day as any for you to learn functions," he said. "Copy down this function for removing bugs from surfaces. Test it on the cellar floor. Then incorporate it into a general cellar-cleaning spell."

Shelly's nose wrinkled in disgust, but she said nothing. The bugs in the cellar creeped her out almost as much as they did Marcus. She knew a punishment when she heard one. As she left to begin her lesson for the day, she resolved to be less exuberant when Marcus was working.

Testing Software

T HE STEWARD STRODE PURPOSEFULLY around the castle's perimeter. His choppy gait propelled him efficiently along the stone path. For anyone else, this excursion would have been a stroll—a chance to walk and think. The steward, however, did not stroll.

As he walked, he replayed the conversation with Hannaldous in his head. A few days before Hannaldous had accidentally cursed the castle, they had met to discuss the final details.

"How are you going to test the spell?" the steward had asked.

Hannaldous's scoff had surprised him. "Wizards never test their spells. It's a waste of time, and our time is valuable."

"I believe testing is a standard practice in the wizarding community," argued the steward. "What of the story of Bianca and the Spell of Moderate Rainfall? It is said that her initial version contained an error in the timing control; a constant was off by a factor of ten. However, she discovered the error by testing the spell on a small patch of land where the Peatbody Swamp is today."

Hannaldous laughed. "Bianca was a junior wizard then, and that was her first major work. She probably had nothing better to do than write a test."

"Surely you should practice this spell on something small first," said the steward. "Why not the royal chicken coop? I am quite certain the chickens would not mind. By now they should have forgotten about the carpenter's last experiment."

Of course, Hannaldous had not been swayed. Wizards were notoriously stubborn.

Now the steward chastised himself for not pushing harder.

Launching an untested spell was reckless; even the steward knew that. Every child in the kingdom had grown up to the tales of Fantastic Freddy, and every child had heard about the untested Spell of Healthy Produce.

Meant to help the farmland, the Spell of Healthy Produce had been a disaster. The town of Ashertoon had seen unimaginable destruction as giant plants tore out of the ground. Asparagus shoots destroyed houses, punching through the foundations and shattering the roofs. The town had finally been abandoned after an eighty-foot pumpkin broke free, flattening three buildings before impaling itself on the corner of city hall with a deafening *splack*. It's said that a two-hundred-foot cornstalk towers over the town to this day.

Muttering to himself, the steward continued his walk.

A curious sight stopped the steward in his tracks and forced his mind back to the present. A smattering of colorful mushrooms dotted the base of the castle's wall. Although they were likely poisonous, the steward had to admit that their bright purple caps added a bit of style to the otherwise grey walls.

The steward glanced around until he found a suitably long stick. Then, with impressive precision, he began knocking mushrooms off the wall. The castle walls were no place for style. Grey was traditional. Grey was impressive.

"Wizards are too busy to test spells," he muttered under his breath as he worked.

His swings came harder and faster. Mushroom caps fell from the walls, forming a beautiful pile in the short grass. The steward made a mental note to send someone to dispose of the pile before the royal pets found it. The pets displayed a consistent lack of common sense when it came to eating random items. Most recently, the king's hedgehog had amazed everyone by consuming nearly a pound of construction gravel.

After a few minutes, the wall was mostly clear of purple fungi. The steward stepped back to survey the work. He knocked away the three surviving mushrooms and nodded with satisfaction.

Then the steward saw the rabbits, and he screamed.

Designing Spells

FOR THE SECOND TIME in three days, Marcus traveled to the capital to meet with the steward. This time, he brought along Shelly, hoping to use the audience as a teaching opportunity.

The steward relayed the latest developments with a barely detectable note of panic. He kept his face impassive and his voice formal, but his eyes betrayed him. Marcus thought that the poor man looked rather stressed.

Purple mushrooms weren't a good sign, but they weren't necessarily a bad sign either. Oddly colored fungi were a common byproduct of sloppy magic. Marcus's own garden held numerous examples—mostly in bright shades of green. One patch of particularly vivid topaz mushrooms served as a reminder not to cast spells before his first cup of coffee.

The rabbits, however, were a problem. Technically, they had nothing to do with the spell itself. They were simply opportunistic. Once they had realized that they could dig into the soft stone, they had set about burrowing. Left unchecked, they would eventually wind tunnels throughout the entire outer wall.

"I suggest hawks," Marcus said.

"Hawks?" asked the steward. "Why not a magical solution? Surely there must be something you can do."

Marcus shook his head. "The castle's condition is too fragile, and I still don't know the depth of Hannaldous's spell. I wouldn't risk adding more magic. Further, the rabbits may have interacted with the magic. They've been burrowing in cursed stone, after all. That can't be good for them. For all I know, a vanishing spell might give them fangs."

The steward's eyes widened in shock.

"In the meantime," Marcus continued, "the rabbits are weakening the walls. Hawks should scare them away and buy us some more time. You can use another bird of prey if you prefer. I don't have any strong feelings there. Hawks were just the first bird that came to mind, after sparrows—but I don't expect sparrows will be much help in scaring away rabbits."

The steward gave a stiff nod. "I shall see to it at once. On the matter of time, how is your progress on the reverse spell?"

Shelly, who had been standing quietly to the side, looked up. She had spent the last two days listening to nonstop complaints about Hannaldous's spell. Marcus could see her brace for another diatribe, which annoyed him further.

"Not well, I'm afraid," said Marcus. "I'm having difficulty deciphering the original spell. It appears Hannaldous never learned to design spells correctly."

For the briefest instant, the steward looked uncertain. "Despite this most recent incident, I believe that Hannaldous has successfully designed many spells in the past," he said. It obviously pained him to defend Hannaldous.

"He wrote spells," Marcus agreed. "But there's a difference between writing a spell down and designing a spell."

Again the steward pushed, "But surely there must have been some design. The spell is hundreds of pages in length. It's incredibly complex."

"The problem does require a complex spell, but nothing nearly this complex," Marcus explained. "In this case, the spell's length is another symptom of poor design. The number of instructions shouldn't be confused with the spell's quality. Whenever possible, you should prefer simplicity and avoid unnecessary complexity. I've seen five-line spells so beautiful they almost made me cry. This spell makes me cry for completely different reasons.

"The basic point, though," Marcus continued, "is that a complex spell needs structure. It needs to be designed.

"Think about a birdhouse," Marcus suggested. "The best

architects will spend months drawing out careful blueprints before the carpenters cut the first piece of wood. They have to design the birdhouse—create a structure to work from. Otherwise, you end up with another royal chicken coop mistake. And it's a lot more work to patch up bad designs after the fact, plus the end result is never as high quality."

"I've seen you write spells without designing them," said Shelly. She immediately clapped her hands to her mouth and turned bright red.

Marcus turned toward his apprentice. He took a deep breath, stifled the urge to yell at her, and smiled.

"It depends on the size and complexity of the spell," Marcus said. "It's true that I don't spend much time designing small spells. I can write a ten-line spell from start to finish without worrying about structure. I can often cast a five-line spell without even writing it down.

"But, for larger spells, I design them first. I might even prototype a few different approaches. A fast prototype can provide invaluable insight into the problem.

"And for something this large," Marcus gestured to the castle all around them. "You need multiple levels of design."

"Levels?" asked the steward.

"Levels of design," confirmed Marcus while mentally searching for an appropriate example.

"Consider the Spell of Mirroring, which I use to back up my notebooks," offered Marcus. "Before I wrote the spell, I had to design it carefully. At a high level, I decided to use a simple approach that syncs out data every ten seconds. To reduce the overhead, the spell only communicates the changes since the last update.

"Given this high-level design, I needed four modules: a magical timer, a module to compute changes, a module to handle communication, and a module to merge in the changes at the other end."

Marcus produced a piece of chalk from his pocket and drew a

simple diagram on a nearby wooden table. The steward's mouth scrunched into a hard line, but he didn't interrupt.

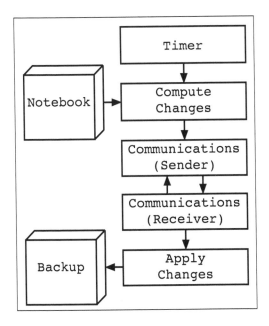

"I also specified the interface between the modules. Here I focused on making the interfaces simple, keeping the intermodule connections to a minimum, and hiding internal information. That way, I could focus on writing each module individually and only worry about their interactions through the defined interfaces.

"Then, of course, I wrote the modules themselves. The magical timer was especially finicky, but most satisfying."

"That seems like a lot of work," said Shelly. "What if you had gotten to the implementation and found a problem with the structure? Then you would've wasted all that time."

"It's the opposite," explained Marcus, while also planning out his later 'discussion' on manners with Shelly. "A good design helps you avoid problems, because you are planning the spell in advance.

"Writing a spell without designing it is like trying to plan a five-course meal while you're already cooking. Before you're done, you find yourself with an undercooked lamb, too many radishes, and no soup course. Tears might also be involved, depending on the exact circumstances."

"I have seen it happen," agreed the steward solemnly.

The group stood in silence, contemplating the image. Shelly shuddered.

"We should be off," Marcus said, returning to the task at hand. "There's work to be done."

The steward nodded. "Thank you for your time. I look forward to your continued progress."

"I'm always at your service," responded Marcus.

Two minutes later, Marcus and Shelly walked across the drawbridge, heading back toward the lab.

"Back to the scroll?" asked Shelly.

"Not yet," answered Marcus. "If I'm going to make any progress, I need more information. I need to go see Agatha."

Shelly stopped. "Agatha? The woman who talks to worms?" she asked.

"She's a powerful wizard, if a bit odd," said Marcus as he continued to walk. "And you will show her the respect that she deserves. While I allow a level of informality in the workshop, you must use her correct title and refer to her as Wizard Agatha."

Shelly jogged to catch up with him again.

"But she talks to worms," she said.

"That's no excuse for informality," said Marcus.

Shelly felt her face flush. "I understand, sir," she said.

Marcus continued, "Agatha has learned to embrace her new bond with the worms, and it's that particular talent I need."

"You need to talk to worms?" asked Shelly.

"Yes," said Marcus.

They walked in silence for another quarter mile before Shelly noticed that they were heading in the wrong direction. "If we're going to see Agatha, then why are we walking toward New Atlantis and the workshop?"

"We'll have to wait until tomorrow to see her," Marcus answered. "She keeps a unique schedule these days. I doubt she'd be up now."

"Isn't there a saying about an early worm?" asked Shelly.

"You shouldn't joke about such things," Marcus responded severely.

Marcus could see the shocked look on her face, but he didn't bother to explain. There are some things that can't be understood until you've spent time with a wizard that speaks to worms.

After a minute of silence, Marcus spoke, "Anyway, there's much to do before we go. I need you to go shopping. Pick up three loaves of bread from Breadista's shop, a dozen eggs from the chicken wrangler, and a fresh cask of orange juice. *No* pulp! I hate chewing my juice in the morning."

"Breadista's?" asked Shelly, panic seeping into her voice.

Marcus looked at her.

"Of course," said Marcus. "He has the best bread. Is there a problem?"

"It's just that Breadista's shop is the opposite direction from the chicken district. Sir Loaf is much closer."

Marcus sighed. "Sir Loaf is a low-quality chain baker. His bread is made at a factory in Turington, frozen, and shipped in. And he doesn't carry raisin loaf."

Shelly opened her mouth to argue but then hesitated. Marcus made an exasperated gesture. "Fine. I'll stop at Breadista's myself. I need to go out and pick up some potion ingredients anyway."

The Dangers of Bad Names

MARCUS WAITED IN FRONT of the apothecary's counter for a full minute before noisily clearing his throat.

"Excuse me. I'm looking for powdered rose petals," said Marcus.

"On the shelf behind you," replied the young clerk without looking up. He continued to copy text onto a sheet of parchment.

Marcus turned and studied the shelf again. A quick search confirmed the lack of powdered rose petals. Marcus turned back to the clerk.

"I didn't see it there," responded Marcus. "In fact, I didn't see any ingredients I recognize. Everything seems to be encoded."

"Shortened," said the clerk.

Before Marcus could ask for clarification, the clerk hopped off his stool and walked around the counter. He proceeded to the nearest shelf, selected a small bottle, and returned to the counter. He placed the bottle on the counter.

"That will be three copper pieces," said the clerk.

Marcus studied the bottle. In large letters, the label stated: "RP3p". He picked up the bottle and turned it over in his hands, searching for other markings. There were none.

"Are you sure this is powdered rose petals?" Marcus asked.

"Oh yes," the clerk said. "This one clearly states 'RP3p,' which means 'rose petals powdered.'"

"I see. You abbreviated it. RP for rose petals and p for powdered. But why the 3?" asked Marcus.

"There's more than one ingredient that can be abbreviated as RP," answered the clerk. "RP1 is raspberry puree, RP2 is red pollen, RP3 is rose petals, and so forth."

"Rotten prunes?" asked Marcus.

"RP10," answered the clerk.

"Rodent pellets?"

"RP9."

"Raw power?"

"Uh ... I don't think we carry that."

"That system is terribly confusing," said Marcus.

"It's my own scheme. It's more efficient," the clerk explained.

"More efficient? You have to figure out awkward abbreviations in order to understand anything," objected Marcus. "It's a wonder that anyone can find what they need."

"The abbreviations all make sense," responded the clerk. "They're all quite simple. How else would you abbreviate rose petals?"

"I wouldn't!" answered Marcus. "I would label each ingredient with its proper name."

"But that's so tedious," complained the young clerk. "Every day, I copy down the names of hundreds of potions I sell to patrons. I have to do that all by hand. Do you know how much faster it is to copy potions with this new system? I save hours."

"My word!" exclaimed Marcus. "You sell potions that use this idiotic encoding? Are you serious?"

The clerk didn't respond.

"Do you know how dangerous that is?" argued Marcus. "What if one of your customers confuses rose petals and rabbit pellets? It could be a disaster! The smell alone could clear out four city blocks."

"But it's more efficient," protested the clerk.

"For you—and at the moment," countered Marcus. "But it makes the potion recipes harder to understand. Worse, it makes it easier to make mistakes."

"The abbreviations are shorter," tried the clerk.

Marcus shook his head. "I know it seems faster and more efficient now, but there's a high price for using such shortcuts. It's better to use clear names. Trust me. I have confused ingredients before; it never ends well."

"You have?" asked the clerk.

"I once copied down a recipe with S for Salt. Unfortunately, three weeks later, I mistakenly read it as Sulfur. S for sulfur seems quite reasonable, right? Needless to say, the omelets tasted terrible—completely inedible."

The clerk appeared at a loss. His face contorted as he searched for a new argument to justify the time savings. Finally, he admitted defeat. "I guess I could change them back."

"You should," encouraged Marcus. "Now, are you absolutely sure that this is the ingredient I need?"

The clerk hesitated.

"I see," said Marcus. "I'll be back some other time, then."

And with that, Marcus left the store. He turned down a side street and started for the Potion Ingredients Plus shop on the other side of town. It was a long walk and the prices were higher, but he needed to be certain that he had the correct ingredients. The last time he had incorrectly mixed up a batch of magic soap, he had smelled like skunk for a week. There were some things on which he refused to take any chances.

Version Control

MARCUS LOVED THE CHALLENGE of developing new spells. He loved breaking problems into components, creating solutions, and combining them into a single coherent spell. It could take him months to perfect a spell to solve a difficult problem. That complexity was why Marcus firmly believed in the importance of version control.

At the end of every day, he would have his apprentice copy his current spell onto a fresh roll of parchment. The apprentice would label the parchment with that day's date and file it in a special drawer. Because of this, if Marcus ever needed access to an old version of his work, he could simply retrieve the correct parchment. Copying scrolls wasn't glamorous work, but Marcus considered it a valuable learning opportunity for the apprentice.

Later that night, as he handed Shelly his latest notes on Hannaldous's spell, she sighed loudly. It was a dramatic, put-upon sigh meant to prompt questions of "What's wrong?" or even "Are you okay?" She felt it delivered the perfect blend of exhaustion (45%), depression (35%), and ennui (20%). She had been practicing.

Marcus ignored her.

Shelly started complaining anyway. "Why do I have to keep copying your spells? You have everything in your notebook already, and you're going to change it again tomorrow. Like this paragraph on mixing the potion—yesterday, I copied almost the exact same thing, except today you crossed out 'Stir 3 times clockwise' and replaced it with 'Stir 4 times counterclockwise.' Why did I bother copying it yesterday? Why can't I wait until you're finished?"

"Two reasons," Marcus began. He enjoyed explaining the logic behind good spell development almost as much as he enjoyed spell development itself. "First, for safety. Do you remember last month when I accidentally set the room on fire? I had been working on the spell to cure dry skin. My lab notebook burned up."

"That was an exceptional case," protested Shelly. "How often do you set your notebook on fire? And if you just made copies of the final product, you would never lose a finished spell."

Even as she spoke, Shelly considered her own question. In the time that she had been Marcus's apprentice, he had managed to set five different notebooks on fire. Maybe he did have a point about backing up his work.

"I would have still lost days of valuable work!" exclaimed Marcus. "A complex spell might take months to develop. It's simply not worth the risk."

"Wait. Aren't you already using a magic mirroring spell on your notebook?" asked Shelly.

Marcus smiled. "Yes. I mirror all my notebooks to a castle out in the country. But there's another reason to copy my notes: developing a spell isn't always a straight-line process. Sometimes, I make mistakes and need to go back to what I did before."

Shelly looked confused.

"Remember when you copied the spell for silencing marching bands?" Marcus asked.

Shelly nodded. Of all the spells she had seen Marcus develop, that was her favorite. She had experimented with it during her brother's high school bocce game. In the middle of a song, the instruments had gone silent. It had been wondrous. Of course, Shelly still felt guilty that she hadn't bothered to learn the reverse spell.

"While I was developing that spell, I changed a section at the end," continued Marcus. "I removed all of the instructions for using the wand and started over. I threw out two weeks' worth of work."

Shelly remembered clearly. She had muttered a lot of nasty

things under her breath when she had seen the paragraphs crossed out.

"Then what happened?" asked Marcus.

Shelly thought back. "You put the instructions back in a few days later."

"Yes!" agreed Marcus. "It turns out that I hadn't factored the wind into the spell. I was able to modify the wording instead. The original wand instructions were fine."

Marcus stared off into space and smiled as though reliving one of the great moments of his life. Shelly's recollection of the events involved less smiling and more muttering.

"I don't understand," said Shelly.

"Version control allows you to go back and recover previous versions," explained Marcus. "If I change my mind and alter an instruction, I cross it out in my notebook. It's gone from my notebook and the mirrored copies. But I might need to go back and look at the old version."

"Why not keep everything in the current notebook?" asked Shelly. "You could add comments saying 'Don't do this' or 'Ignore this' so that you know which instructions are old. That way you never need to throw anything out."

"That would be too messy, like Hannaldous's spell," argued Marcus. "Version control is cleaner. I can make whatever changes I want, and I know that I can always go back to a previous version if I need it."

"But …" started Shelly, but she had run out of arguments. She could remember many instances when Marcus had made major changes to a spell, only to backtrack the next day. During the development of the Spell of Singing Rocks, he had introduced a critical bug in both the pitch and the volume controls during one revision. As the rocks belted out a shrill rendition of "We Will Rock You," she had sprinted to the file cabinet to retrieve the spell's previous version.

"But … my hand hurts from copying the same instructions over and over," Shelly finally admitted.

Marcus tried to look sympathetic. "I know it can be a tiresome task. That's why I have apprentices do it for me."

Shelly didn't feel any better.

Debugging

A T A LITTLE AFTER six the next morning, Marcus and Shelly set off to visit Agatha. She lived on an abandoned farm in the outskirts of Grassford. The grounds provided an expansive home to the families of worms she supported. Rumor had it that Agatha spent most of her days running through the fields to scare away birds.

"How does she talk to them? The worms, I mean," Shelly asked after they had walked a few miles.

"Magic," replied Marcus.

Shelly rolled her eyes. "I knew that. It has to be magic. I've never heard of anyone born with the ability to talk to anything smaller than an fanged mountain turtle, and I think that's an old myth.

"And why?" Shelly pressed. "Who casts a spell to talk to worms?"

Marcus said nothing.

"Oh!" exclaimed Shelly as a thought struck her. "Is it a curse? Did someone curse her?"

Marcus stopped walking and turned to her. His face was hard.

"Agatha was not cursed," he said. "And you should be careful how you discuss her ... situation. She can be sensitive about it."

"Oh. Sorry," Shelly mumbled.

Marcus nodded and continued walking. After a minute of silence, he spoke again. "It was an accident."

Shelly glanced over. Marcus stared at the ground as he walked, seemingly mesmerized by the speckling of rocks in the dirt.

When Marcus didn't continue, she asked, "An accident?"

"Agatha was perhaps the most talented student in my year," said Marcus. "We were apprentices with Wizard Calciate at the same time. She mastered every spell effortlessly. She even excelled at spell design. She was amazing.

"Then, things fell apart. That spell was supposed to give her the ability to talk to small woodland creatures like chipmunks or squirrels. Unfortunately, she overshot. She gained the ability to speak with worms, lice, and flies. For obvious reasons, she prefers to spend her time talking to worms."

"Oh," said Shelly.

Marcus shrugged. "She insists that she's thrilled with the results," he said. "But she has been a little … off since the spell."

"I see," said Shelly. "And her talent will help us now?"

"I hope so," said Marcus.

"How?"

"We need to find out what went wrong with the spell, and it's too late for debugging, I'm afraid."

"Debugging?"

"An advanced form of magic," Marcus said. His face brightened as he spoke. "Magical debuggers allow you to step through a spell as it executes. This allows you to examine the interior variables of the spell as they change. You can see what's happening as the spell unfolds."

"You watch a spell execute with extra information?" asked Shelly. "That must be like flipping through a dictionary. There would be a ton of information flying past in a blur. How could that possibly help?"

Marcus laughed. "I assure you, it's better than that. Debugging allows you to step through a spell. You can pause after each action and watch how it unfolds.

"Think about the Spell of Bread De-Staling, where you turn a rock-hard loaf of bread into something edible. After the initial chants and the flash of light, what happens?"

Shelly groped around in her head for an answer. Finally, she settled on the obvious. "The bread becomes un-stale?"

"Yes. But what really happens?"

"I'm not sure," Shelly admitted. "It happens so fast. I figured it was just magic."

"It is magic, but many steps of magic. First the spell flows into the bread. You can see the location of the spell change. Then the spell shifts moisture around inside the bread. It looks much like a WHILE loop. With a debugger, you can track the internal state of the bread at each step."

"Really?" asked Shelly.

Marcus stopped walking and rummaged in his pockets. Eventually, he produced an old biscuit. He wasn't sure why it had been in his pocket or how long it had been there, but it was perfect for his demonstration. He tapped on it to confirm its rock-like staleness.

Then he spoke quietly for a while, making a few precise movements with his hand.

"Watch," he said.

Marcus started to perform the Spell of Bread De-Staling. Glowing information popped into existence above the biscuit, like a tiny holographic scoreboard.

"Wow," said Shelly.

She read the information labeled in the tiny infographic:

```
LoopIteration = 0
MoistureContent = 0.1
AirSpeed = 1.33
```

"I'll step forward one iteration of the loop," said Marcus.
The information changed:

```
LoopIteration = 1
MoistureContent = 0.2
AirSpeed = 1.38
```

"And another iteration," said Marcus.

```
LoopIteration = 2
MoistureContent = 0.3
AirSpeed = 1.45
```

"What do you see?" he asked.

"The loop iteration is increasing and the moisture content is going up," said Shelly. She leaned in closer to the floating text.

"What else?" asked Marcus as he advanced the spell another step.

```
LoopIteration = 3
MoistureContent = 0.4
AirSpeed = 1.51
```

"The air speed is increasing," said Shelly, sounding unsure.

"Exactly," said Marcus. With a wave of his hand the debugger stopped and the infographic disappeared. "Few wizards ever notice that the air moves faster around the bread, but it's essential for the spell. The bread constantly needs new air to provide moisture, so the spell has to cycle the air around the target. You can tell a lot about whether the spell is working from the Air-Speed variable alone."

"Wow," said Shelly again. Her eyes grew wide as she thought about the implications. "So much information," she breathed. "It could take forever to step through a long spell, though. Something like the Spell of Extra Butter could take years."

"You don't have to step through every action," Marcus assured her. "You can set breakpoints in your spell. The spell will chug along until it hits a breakpoint. Then it will stop and let you step through. You can set it going again until the next breakpoint whenever you want."

"That seems useful," said Shelly.

"Admittedly, using magical debugging isn't terribly exciting when the spell goes according to plan," said Marcus. "But it's invaluable for understanding what's happening inside a broken spell. As I recall, you could have used more information about the state variables of the kitchen mop during last week's exercise."

Shelly recalled the fleeing puddles. She still had no idea what had gone wrong.

"Can you teach me?" asked Shelly.

"When you're ready."

"How about the castle? Can I watch the debugging?"

"Unfortunately, it's too late for debugging," replied Marcus. "In this case, we must resort to worms."

"Deworming then?" asked Shelly.

Marcus gave a dry laugh. "It's too late to observe the spell in action," he explained. "So we have to poke around at what's left and try to piece together what happened. The worms will help us inspect the walls' current state. With any luck, there will be something left—a residual cruft that Hannaldous forgot to clean up."

"It doesn't sound as good as debugging," said Shelly.

"Oh, it isn't. It's like trying to understand what happened to a ship based on the shipwreck. You lose vital information about what happened during the accident."

By this point, they had reached the dirt lane leading to Agatha's farm. Shelly noticed a worried look cross Marcus's face as he turned up the lane toward the farmhouse. He hurriedly brushed the traveling dust from his cloak.

They walked onto a small porch, where Marcus wiped his feet twice before proceeding to the door. He knocked. Inside, Shelly could hear the shuffle of someone moving.

Marcus leaned close to Shelly and whispered in her ear, "Whatever you do, don't make any worm jokes." His breath smelled unusually minty.

When the door opened, Marcus's eyes lit up brighter than Shelly had thought possible.

"Agatha!" he exclaimed. "It's amazing to see you again."

Comments

Marcus, Shelly, and Agatha stood in the castle's courtyard. Shelly stared up at the high castle walls, alternately in awe of their heights and terrified that they would come crashing down. Behind her, Agatha slowly paced the yard while staring at the ground. Marcus waited off to the side, occupying himself with a scroll that Agatha had given him.

"This spell is a breath of fresh air," said Marcus.

"You like it?" asked Agatha. "I've been working at it for a while. Many wiggly bits to sort out."

Shelly shuddered at the description but remained silent. In the last two hours, Agatha had primarily used terminology suited for worms. All descriptions incorporated some form of the words *wiggling* or *dirt*. In Agatha's opinion, these were generally applicable terms. As awkward as this was, however, deciphering the conversation turned out to be less difficult than Shelly would have imagined.

"I would imagine," Marcus said. "The subspell for checking the moisture alone appears quite challenging."

"Can't let the dirt get dry," responded Agatha. As she spoke, she lowered herself onto the ground and pressed her ear against the dirt.

"It's more than the difficulty or the structure," continued Marcus, oblivious to her actions. His eyes remained glued on the scroll. "The spell is readable—wonderfully readable. And your comments are great."

"Gotta do that," Agatha remarked from her position on the ground. "In a big enough patch of dirt, all the rocks look alike.

You gotta leave signs in the ground to tell you where you've been and what you were thinking. Otherwise, you get all confused, like a slug." She laughed loudly at her own joke.

Agatha lifted her head, shifted it three inches to the left, and pressed it firmly back to the ground.

"Shelly, look at this," said Marcus.

Shelly tore her eyes away from Agatha's strange activity and looked at the scroll. Lines of green text were interspersed with large blocks of neat black instructions.

"What are the green lines?" asked Shelly. Her eyes darted back to Agatha, who was tapping on the ground with three fingers and humming.

"Comments," answered Marcus. "Descriptions within the spell to provide additional explanation or context. Comments are the things I keep telling you to add to your spells."

"Oh, right," said Shelly. "Are they really necessary, though?"

On the ground, Agatha rolled onto her back and closed her eyes.

"Absolutely," answered Marcus. "Comments help provide context for other readers. Take this line for example: 'Soften the rabbit pellets.' That comment explains the reason for the next ten instructions of adding water, heating, and stirring."

"So you add comments when someone else is going to read your scroll?" asked Shelly. "I guess that makes sense. If you had to do it all the time, it would add a lot of work."

Agatha continued to lie on the ground with her eyes closed. She had resumed the tapping, but now opted for only two fingers.

"It's not just for other readers," said Marcus. "Compare the instructions you just read to this."

Marcus produced another scroll from his bag. Shelly recognized it as one of her first assignments—a spell for making lemonade stir itself. She barely remembered writing it.

"What does this instruction do?" Marcus asked.

Shelly squinted at the text. The lines read "5a) Examine each sugar cube. 5b) Select the heaviest one that has not already been selected. 5c) Move the selected cube to a new location behind the previously selected cubes. 5d) Repeat 5a – 5c as needed."

"Umm …" Shelly stalled as she tried to remember what those lines meant.

"Umm … Umm … Ohm … Ohm …" Agatha took up the chant from the ground.

"It …" Shelly continued to stall.

"It sorts the sugar cubes by weight," Marcus finished for her. "That's the value of comments—they provide critical information. Even if you understand a spell perfectly when you write it, that doesn't mean you'll remember it. Comments preserve knowledge and context."

"You never recognize the dirt you wiggled past last week," added Agatha.

"Exactly," said Marcus. "I think."

"You know who didn't use comments?" Marcus prompted.

Shelly wanted to groan. It all came back to this. "Hannaldous," she recited.

"Precisely," said Marcus. "And now we're sitting outside the castle waiting for the worms to help."

At that statement, Agatha opened her eyes and propped herself up on her elbows. She blinked at them a few times as her eyes readjusted to the light. "Oh. The worms already helped. I was just chatting with them while you finished your little teaching moment."

"Splendid," said Marcus. "What did they say?"

"They were happy to help—happier than a Snarzari flatworm in fresh dung. They said there were a bunch of strange things about the wall: the rock feels grainy, everything tastes like lemons, the moisture content is two-thirds of normal, there is a lack of feldspar, and there is a low humming."

As she spoke, Marcus noted the observations in a small notebook. "How about a vinegary smell?" he asked.

"Yeah. Mostly in the weaker parts of the wall," said Agatha.

"Which are where?" asked Marcus.

"The lower levels on the east side. It seems the damage tunneled out from there. Undulated all the way up to the west turret. But, still, it's not as bad there."

"I see."

"I assume you know about the rabbits," Agatha said.

"Yes," said Marcus.

"Quite odd behavior if you ask me," said Agatha. "I would expect it from chipmunks—you can't trust them. But not from rabbits. It's plain odd for rabbits."

Marcus made a few more notes before looking up. "Thank you, Agatha. This has been very helpful. Unfortunately, we need to go back to the workshop now. Would you like to join us?"

"No thanks," Agatha said, flopping back to the ground. "The worms were just telling me some juicy gossip about the last garden party. It appears that there was a bit of a scene involving spilled champagne and a tipsy duchess."

"I imagine that would be quite exciting for them," said Marcus. "Well, thank you again."

With that, Marcus and Shelly left Agatha with her ear pressed to the ground. As the path rounded a hedge, Shelly heard Agatha burst out giggling.

Best Practices

MARCUS AND SHELLY WALKED back to the lab in silence. A thousand questions swirled through Shelly's head.

"You're too quiet," Marcus said.

It was the first time she had ever heard him say that.

"Granted, I'm not complaining," he added. "I enjoy the silence. It's just worrying. If you have something to say, I suggest you come out and say it."

"It's Agatha," Shelly admitted.

"What about her?" prompted Marcus.

"She talks to worms," Shelly said, more to fill the gap than anything else.

"I know," responded Marcus.

They walked another hundred feet before Shelly spoke again.

"Could you reverse the spell?" she asked.

"Perhaps," said Marcus, his voice far away. "It wouldn't do any good, though. As Agatha herself told me, once you see the world through a worm's eyes, you can't see it any other way. Plus, Agatha doesn't want to give up her … gift."

Shelly thought about this. "I thought worms didn't have eyes," she said.

"They don't," agreed Marcus. "But Agatha sees her worms differently than we do. She once claimed her worms have a discerning taste for dirt and proceeded to lecture me on the maximum sand content of comfortable garden soil."

"But she wasn't always like that," Shelly said. "I don't understand why you don't help her. I can tell how you feel—" The words rushed out before she could stop them.

"That's enough," Marcus interrupted. He didn't raise his voice, but his tone was clear.

Marcus's face was hard when he spoke again. "I've offered, many times. But Agatha isn't interested in reversing the spell."

"But—" started Shelly.

"There are no buts," said Marcus. "I will not cast a counterspell on someone without a good reason, and Agatha doesn't want me to perform a counterspell."

Shelly didn't know what else to say.

Marcus continued after a minute, "Have I told you how she came upon her gift?"

"You said she was trying to talk to animals and she overshot," answered Shelly.

"Indeed," said Marcus. "She considers it a fortuitous accident. In my opinion, she made an unnecessary and costly mistake. She simply chanted one too many times."

"She chanted an extra time?" asked Shelly.

"An off-by-one error in a loop—very similar to miscounting. Sadly, it's all too common."

Shelly was shocked. Of all the mistakes to make, this seemed easily avoidable. She said as much to Marcus.

"It was," he agreed. "But Agatha had gotten arrogant. She refused to test her potions, she was sloppy about variable names, and she left out all comments. In short, she neglected all of the best practices of spell creation."

"I thought you said she was talented," said Shelly, trying to piece together the story.

"Talent alone isn't enough," said Marcus. "You must adhere to good spell design practices. Even the most talented wizards can get careless and sloppy. Most of the time the result is simply annoying—a lab catches on fire or a spell fizzles. Agatha learned the hard way."

Shelly couldn't think of anything to say, and the rest of the journey passed in silence.

Unit Tests

"**T**HIS IS BORING," ANNOUNCED Shelly the next morning as she read the day's assignment. The Spell of Napkin Folding consisted of five short instructions. "When can I learn something interesting? When can I do real magic? What about the Spell of Debugging?"

"You have to master the fundamentals first," Marcus insisted. Still frustrated by the lack of progress on Hannaldous's spell, he was in no mood to argue.

"I already know the fundamentals," Shelly responded.

Marcus sighed. In his day, an apprentice didn't argue with his or her master. You listened, and you were respectful. Why was everyone so impatient? Marcus blamed the latest pop culture fad: marching bands. Sadly, there was only one way to reinforce the fundamentals.

"Okay," Marcus responded. "You can do the Spell of Transmogrified Mold, which transforms ordinary house mold into candy. It's a complex spell that requires six potions and three hours. Can you handle that?"

"Yes!" agreed Shelly, visibly bouncing with excitement.

Marcus smiled as he handed her the directions. "Here you go. There should be plenty of mold in the kitchen. I believe a certain apprentice hasn't cleaned there in weeks."

Ignoring the comment, Shelly ran off to the kitchen to begin the spell.

The key to the Spell of Transmogrified Mold is correctly making each of the six potions. If any one of the potions is off by even a little, the final product is a complete failure. Granted, the result will still look, taste, and smell like chocolate. However, it will cause three hours of intense nausea and powerful hiccups. Together, those turn out to be a most unpleasant combination.

While Shelly buzzed around the kitchen, Marcus decided to take a nap. He had been up half the night trying to decipher a particularly scrunched patch of writing. The dancing candlelight had made the task difficult, and he had admitted defeat at half past three.

As he retired to a quiet back room, he paused briefly. There was no need to remind Shelly to test each potion individually. By this point in her training, the value of testing should be ingrained.

Marcus himself had learned the value of unit tests early in his apprenticeship. Once he had spent ten days tracking down a subtle bug in a levitation spell before Wizard Calciate had scolded him, "If you had written unit tests for your functions, you could have quickly and thoroughly ensured their correctness. Now you are flailing around, trying to fix a twenty-page spell."

Of course, young apprentices always complained that testing their potions slowed them down. In fact, they often complained about all forms of testing. But sometimes there was only one way to learn the value of best practices.

Three hours later, Marcus awoke to the sound of loud vomiting. "I believe she's done," he mumbled to himself as he made his way to the kitchen.

There he found Shelly with her head in a bucket.

"How did it go?" he asked.

"I don't know what went wrong," moaned Shelly between hiccups.

"Let me see," offered Marcus. He wandered over to the counter and started testing the potions.

The first three were correct.

"Ah. Too much vinegar in the fourth potion. Common mistake. My guess is that you didn't notice because there's also too much salt in the last potion. Yep. There it is. All very common."

"They all looked correct," Shelly protested between powerful hiccups. "And the end result seemed to work out."

"Yes. But the potions were wrong," noted Marcus.

Shelly tried to respond but fell into a prolonged bout of vomiting.

"You'll be fine in another two hours and fifty-three minutes. Until then, I would recommend keeping a bucket close," Marcus advised. He patted her shoulder awkwardly in an attempt to be reassuring.

On his way out, he paused at the door. "Remember what I told you yesterday about Agatha and best practices?" he asked.

Shelly groaned and hiccuped. Another dry heave followed.

Marcus continued, "In the future, I encourage you to thoroughly test each individual component of a spell. Unit tests are important. You need to make sure the fundamentals are correct before building on them. Otherwise, you can find unpleasant surprises."

Meaningful Names

A FEW DAYS LATER, SHELLY sat in the New Atlantis Mall's food court, picking at an overpriced blueberry muffin. Her best friend, Veronica, watched her from across the table. Veronica stared at Shelly's blueberry muffin, her curiosity shifting to concern. As a near fanatic of any food containing blueberries, Veronica simply couldn't understand Shelly's untouched snack.

"Have you told Marcus about Ivan's muffins yet?" asked Veronica, snapping Shelly out of her thoughts.

"No," Shelly said. She could feel the rush of heat to her face. Then, after a deep breath, she continued, "I don't plan to, either. There's no reason he has to know about it."

"What if Breadista tells him?" asked Veronica.

"Ivan would have to tell Breadista, and I don't see that happening. Ivan's probably worried about getting into trouble."

"That's dumb," said Veronica. "Why should he get into trouble? It was all your fault."

Veronica wasn't known for being sympathetic.

"Marcus is already in a foul mood anyway," Shelly continued, staring at her uneaten muffin. "It's that stupid spell. I don't want to add any more stress."

"No luck yet?" asked Veronica.

Shelly shook her head. "The spell is a complete mess—almost impossible to understand. It actually had a subspell named Do-Stuff. It's the only function in the entire spell, of course. Can you believe that name? How are you supposed to figure out what Do-Stuff does?"

"Magic stuff," answered Veronica in complete seriousness.

"What is stuff?" Shelly asked. "The name is completely meaningless. It doesn't say anything about what the subspell actually does."

"But it sounds magical," said Veronica.

"No, it doesn't," argued Shelly. "And names shouldn't be magical; they should be meaningful. Subspells' names should be verb phrases that indicate what a spell does, like MixPotion or TestWindSpeed. Variable names should be nouns that indicate what the variable stores, like totalFrogCount or weightOfMold. Nothing should be as vague as 'stuff.'"

"Take the Spell of Excessive Tartness," Shelly continued. "It can turn the juiciest blueberry into a face-scrunchingly tart surprise. It has three subspells: MeasureAcidity, MeasureBlueberries, and ReduceSweetness. Can you guess what they do?"

"Measure the acidity, measure the number of blueberries, and reduce the sweetness," said Veronica.

"Exactly," said Shelly. "They perform actions, and their names are verb phrases describing the actions. Their use is clear, which makes the whole spell easier to understand."

Shelly looked off into space and gave a dry laugh. "The first time I copied the spell, I shortened the measuring functions to Measure1 and Measure2. Marcus gave me an earful about that. 'How are you supposed to know what they measure?' he said.

"And then there's a name like DoStuff. What stuff is it supposed to be doing?"

"But ..." stammered Veronica. "Who would want to make a blueberry tart on purpose?"

Shelly ignored her question. "Can you imagine if you had to deal with stupid terms every day in your job? What if the tax forms had a space for 'value' without any other information?"

"That would be unacceptable," Veronica said, emphasizing each word. She didn't joke about accounting. "Unlike magic, accounting is *not* a field for ambiguity. How would you know what value to put there?"

Shelly shrugged. "Maybe it's for the sum of all revenue."

"Then it should be labeled **Sum of Revenue**," said Veronica. Shelly could almost hear the Sans Serif font in Veronica's tone.

"Do you think accountants are just cavalier number jockeys?" asked Veronica. "Simon T. Flutternick's second maxim of accounting states: 'All entries shall be clearly labeled.' It's one of the foundational principles of modern accounting."

"I—" started Shelly, but it was too late.

"Two hundred years ago, the City of New Atlantis almost fell into bankruptcy because of a field labeled **Result**. **Result** stored gross adjusted income, but, ten pages later, the form's creator thought it was net income. Do you realize how much confusion that caused? If he had only labeled it **Gross Adjusted Income**—"

"I didn't mean to upset you," Shelly interrupted. "I just wanted to point out why Marcus is so annoyed. Names are important in magic too."

"Oh," said Veronica. She nodded slowly, as if still deciding whether she was conceding any points about accounting. The anger drained from her face.

"I guess that sounds pretty bad," said Veronica. "I see why Marcus is in a terrible mood."

"Hannaldous used the variable 'value' nineteen different times in his spell," said Shelly. "One time he's referring to water temperature and another time to number of ants. Marcus hasn't figured out the other seventeen uses yet."

Veronica cringed.

"It's hopeless," mumbled Shelly as she returned to poking the runny blueberries in her muffin.

"Maybe you need a vacation," offered Veronica. "You have time saved up, right? You always talk about going to visit your folks in Alexandria. You could take a few weeks off while Marcus solves the curse."

Shelly shrugged without looking up from her muffin. "Maybe," she said.

Code Reviews

S HELLY NOTICED AN ODD sight as soon as she entered the lab. Marcus's inbox overflowed with letters and scrolls. From the size of it, this pile must have been accumulating for days.

She fingered through the top few items, stopping to examine a lone postcard in the stack. The picture showed a dull green field under a gray, cloudy sky, and the caption read "A vacation that is worth a re-peat." It appeared that Marcus's cousin had been visiting the scenic peat farms of Northandland.

As she flipped the card back into the pile, Shelly realized that, in addition to the normal bills and sales flyers, the pile seemed to be composed largely of scrolls. She even recognized a few return addresses.

"What's with all the mail?" she asked.

"I haven't had a chance to go through it," answered Marcus from his desk. "I've been busy." He gestured at the scroll and his notes.

"I know," said Shelly. "But what is it all?"

"The usual stuff, I expect. Bills, sales flyers, notices from various professional organizations, and spell reviews."

"Spell reviews?" asked Shelly. "Is that like a book review?"

"No, it isn't like a book review. I review the spells for errors, good design, readability, and so forth."

"Why?" asked Shelly.

Marcus set down his quill and turned to face her. "All spells must be reviewed by a senior wizard before they're committed to the official wizards' spellbooks. Spell reviews ensure the correctness and quality of the spells. I'm one of the foremost reviewers in the kingdom."

"Why?" repeated Shelly.

Marcus looked irritated. "Because I command vast magical knowledge and have significant experience writing spells," he explained.

"That's not what I meant," Shelly said hurriedly. She could feel her face flush with embarrassment. "I meant, why do they do spell reviews? It seems like a lot of extra work. Shouldn't wizards wait until their spells are perfect to submit them? Why have someone else check them?"

"What have you learned from Hannaldous's mistake?" asked Marcus. Shelly expected him to continue into another diatribe, but he waited for an answer.

"Umm," she fumbled. "He didn't follow the best practices of spell design."

"Exactly," said Marcus.

Shelly let out a sigh of relief.

Marcus continued, with passion building in his voice, "The official wizards' spellbooks are the ground truth for all wizards. They are the collected knowledge of countless generations. They're copied and stored in ten major libraries across the kingdom. Those spells are used thousands of times by hundreds of wizards. The spells must be high quality!

"Hundreds of years ago, anyone could submit a scroll to the collection. Volumes were filled with unreadable, and often broken, garbage. Each time you used a new spell from the collection, you were gambling your life on the author's skill. Once, the entire Brunswick town square was overrun by fire-breathing frogs due to a single incorrect variable name!

"Then the fourth master librarian, Henry the Mostly Efficient, instituted the spell review process. He decreed that all new spells must be reviewed by another qualified wizard before being recorded in the collection."

"And that worked?" asked Shelly. "The wizards agreed to that?"

The concept struck Shelly as odd. As a rule, wizards hated to admit they were wrong. The thought of them asking other wizards to check their work was shocking.

Marcus laughed. "No," he said. "It took Fantastic Freddy's unfortunate incident with some oversized produce before they would listen. Even then, half the wizards refused. They defected and started their own collections. They didn't last long, though. The Scrolls of Improved Modern Wizardry lasted the longest—eighteen months."

"What happened to them?" asked Shelly.

"Their collections were a mess, of course. Without anyone reviewing the quality of the spells, they filled with garbage. After a few years, almost all the defecting wizards came back.

"Soon enough the wizarding community came around to the idea of spell review. Sure, it adds extra work. But it's worth it.

"It helps to have a second pair of eyes look over a spell. The reviewer brings a fresh perspective that can help catch errors. And having another wizard review the spell ensures that the spell is understandable by others.

"Moreover, the review soon served another purpose: education. Senior wizards would help younger wizards learn by providing helpful reviews. And, in return, the reviewers would learn new tricks from the spells they read.

"It turns out to be a useful system. The key is that everyone has to care about providing useful feedback and submitting high-quality spells. Those two conditions are vital."

"The reviewers check for correctness and readability?" confirmed Shelly.

"Those are the most important factors," said Marcus. "But reviewers comment on a range of programming practices. Unnecessary complexity is another common problem.

"I found two problems in my last spell review for Agatha. The first problem was an off-by-one error; Agatha had used <= when she meant <. The second problem was one of efficiency. I recommended that Agatha initially sort her list of dandelions instead of repeatedly searching through an unsorted list."

Shelly was impressed. Although it seemed like a significant amount of extra work, she could see the value.

"Why didn't that prevent Hannaldous's castle spell?" she asked.

"Because Hannaldous never submitted his spell for review!" answered Marcus, the bitterness accrued over the past ten days returning to his voice. "You're only required to get a review when you submit a spell to the collection. Hannaldous just wrote the spell and cast it."

Shelly looked back at the pile of scrolls in the mail. "So all of those scrolls …?"

"Will have to wait," answered Marcus. "The castle is more important."

"Maybe I could help with them," she offered.

Marcus chuckled. "Not yet. To be a good reviewer, you must have enough experience. You must understand where spells can go wrong and what makes good style. You still have a lot to learn."

Shelly wanted to scream with frustration, but she held it in. Suddenly, the idea of getting away from the lab and the hours of collecting mold was the only thing in her mind. She needed a break from learning the basics. She needed a vacation.

"You know … I have a lot of vacation time saved up, and you're busy with this castle curse …" she began.

Constant Data

P ETER HAD ALMOST CRIED when he found the first vandal-
ized scroll. In his two years as an apprentice at the great Library of Alexandria, he had never had a patron deface a scroll. It
would never happen here, he had convinced himself.

Peter had first noticed the vandalism in a scroll titled *Exciting
and Lucrative Opportunities in Donkey Cart Manufacturing*. Halfway
through the third chapter, someone had edited the instructions.
The phrase "Secure with four nails" had been crossed out and re-
written as "Secure with three nails (that's good enough)."

"How could someone do this?" Peter had wondered aloud, unable to look away from the scroll. Experts had probably spent de-
cades rigorously studying cart construction before committing
their knowledge to this scroll. Defacing it was an insult not just
to their knowledge, but by extension to *all* knowledge.

Peter had imagined that the perpetrator felt justified. They
would have reasoned, quite incorrectly, that they were being
helpful. They might even have been able to put forth an argument about improving knowledge. Peter had felt a ball of rage
in his stomach as he played through hundreds of imaginary
confrontations.

After the third incident of vandalism, a lingering sense of
dread began to haunt Peter. He spent hours of his own time
searching for the miscreant and devising elaborate traps, but
none of it worked. He decided to consult the master librarian.

"It's a sad day indeed," agreed the librarian. "We need to find
out who's doing this and ask them to stop."

"Ask them to stop?" cried Peter. "We need to do something

more than just ask. How about a lifetime ban from the library?"

"Perhaps," the master librarian agreed. "As long as we ban them nicely. This is, after all, a library. We have to maintain our high standards of helpfulness and politeness."

But after finding another two edited scrolls, Peter was too angry to wait.

One night after work, he explained the problem to Shelly, who was an old friend from grade school. Two days into her visit, Peter had already spent hours listening to her complain about her apprenticeship. After listening to one particularly lengthy monologue about "being stuck on the basics," Peter felt justified in complaining about his own graffiti problem.

"Oh! I can help!" Shelly said when he finished.

"How?" Peter asked suspiciously. He had had mixed luck with wizards in the past. A recent experiment had left him unable to clip his fingernails for three months. And, of course, he still had regular nightmares about the NP-hard curse.

"Const Spell of Immutability!" Shelly said.

"Const Spell of Immutability?" asked Peter. This sounded like exactly the type of spell that would end in disaster.

"Const is short for constant," explained Shelly. "The spell makes it impossible to edit written documents. Marking something as constant protects it from accidental or intentional modification. You use it on texts you don't want to change, like legal documents or poems."

"Poems?"

"It happens more than you'd believe," Shelly said. "Poets ask us to cast the const spell on their poems so they're forced to stop fiddling with their work. This one poet was stuck tweaking the same line for ten years before we made the work constant."

"Oh, interesting."

"More often, we use it to mark a variable or the result of a subspell constant. That guarantees it won't be modified before it's used."

"Subspell?" asked Peter, looking confused and more than a

little worried.

"Consider the Spell of Everlasting Candles," explained Shelly. "Before you can make a candle burn forever, you need to cast a small spell to determine the energy in the candle—the Spell of Candle Analysis. You write down the resulting value and use it in the Spell of Everlasting Candles. However, if you *accidentally* change the value by spilling a large mug of tea over your notes, you can end up with a candle that screams when lit.

"Or so I heard," Shelly added.

Peter stared at her.

"Can I use the const spell on your scrolls? Please? I'm so bored. I could really use the practice. I promise I'll be careful," pleaded Shelly.

Peter was about to say no when he glanced down at the scroll in his hands. In the middle of a description of garden care, the helpful patron had noted, "Don't let your dog water the flowers, though. It doesn't work well." Rage filled his belly.

So Peter fought back the images of destruction, fire, and screaming scrolls. He pushed all concerns out of his mind and held them off long enough to agree. The brief gap allowed Peter a blissful two minutes of believing that everything would be fine.

Shelly spent that night wandering around the library casting her spell on the scrolls. It was a slow process. Peter sat behind the desk, watching nervously. He chewed at his fingernails, grateful that they were no longer hard as stone.

When nothing burned, exploded, or screamed, he considered the night a victory.

As Shelly finished, Peter remembered a question that he should have asked earlier.

"What happens if someone tries to modify the scroll?" he asked.

"They can't," answered Shelly.

"I know, but what stops them? A voice in the back of their mind? A force field? A stabbing pain? Annoying music? Please don't let it be annoying music. The library is a place for quiet. Oh no! It's loud music, isn't it?"

"Force field," answered Shelly. She sounded tired. Then again, she had been casting the same spell over and over for hours. Even Peter was exhausted from listening to the same thing all night.

Peter sighed with relief.

The next day, Peter sat behind the main counter of the library, trying hard not to fall asleep. Then, he heard a patron at a nearby desk muttering something. Peter peered over at the man. He was trying to write something on the scroll, but his hand stopped millimeters from the parchment. The man looked confused as he struggled to move the pen closer.

Finally, he shouted something at the parchment that sounded distressingly like "Your loss" and stormed out of the library. Peter smiled to himself; Shelly's const spell had worked.

= V₅ = =

$\mathbf{A}$ s King Fredrick completed his daily inspection of the castle's outer walls, he came to the northern gate. He smiled. Despite the seemingly inevitable doom of his lifelong home, the sight of the northern gate always gave him hope. He remembered sitting on his father's knee, listening to his fiftieth retelling of the Incident at the Northern Gate.

❧❧❧

The Incident at the Northern Gate had occurred while King Fredrick's father, King Henry, held the throne. As part of his effort to improve the castle's operation, King Henry personally oversaw the creation of new rules and procedures.

The guards' new rules for guarding the gate read:

Check each entrant's ID and examine his or her entrance ID class.
- IF (ID class = = 0): the entrant is a member of the royal family, so allow the entrant to pass;
- ELSE IF (ID class = = 1): the entrant is a member of the king's extended family, so consult with the king before allowing the entrant to pass;
- ELSE IF (ID class = = 2): the entrant is a member of the carpenters' guild, so allow the entrant to pass;
- ELSE IF (ID class = = 3): the entrant is a member of the plumbers' guild, so allow the entrant to pass;

and so forth.

Unfortunately, even a king makes syntax errors, although that fact has never been documented by a castle historian.

The erroneous line read:

- ELSE IF (ID class = 72): the entrant is a mime, so stop him/her.

King Henry had used an assignment statement (=) instead of an equality test (= =).

It took almost three hours before anyone reached this test in the series of IF-ELSE statements. Late in the afternoon, a young hedgehog walker (ID class 185) returned from an extended outing with King Henry's prize hedgehog. He presented his ID to the north gate's guard. The guard consulted his manual and paused in confusion.

"What's wrong?" asked the boy.

"Well. The manual says I'm to change your ID class to 72 and prevent you from entering," the guard slowly answered as his brain struggled to rationalize the situation.

Finally, deciding that he never understood the rules anyway, the guard reached into his booth and pulled out a permanent marker. He crossed out the ID class of 185 and wrote 72 in its place.

"But I'm supposed to go inside," argued the boy. "I have the king's hedgehog."

"I'm sorry, lad. No mimes allowed in here!" responded the guard. Now that the ID showed the boy to be a mime, the guard felt confident. He knew how to handle mimes.

The boy looked confused. "Mime?"

"Yes. It says ID class 72. That means you're a mime," answered the guard.

"But you just wrote that. It was ID class 185. I'm a certified hedgehog walker. I provide a valuable public service!"

"The manual told me to reclassify you as a mime, so that's what

I did. And we don't allow mimes here!" responded the guard.

"But—" started the boy.

"Be gone!" shouted the guard. He always enjoyed shouting at mimes. They never shouted back.

The boy retreated and circled around to the south gate. Unfortunately, his ID now clearly indicated that he was a mime. He wasn't allowed to enter. Discouraged, the boy went home, bringing along the king's hedgehog.

The hedgehog walker's absence went unnoticed for most of the day. When King Henry finally realized his hedgehog was missing, he sent out a search party. Fifty knights arrived at the boy's home, scaring both the boy and the hedgehog out of their wits. It took three hours for the boy to pull himself together enough to explain what had happened. It took another five hours to calm down the hedgehog, who had wedged himself firmly in a shoe.

The king was furious when he found out. He marched down to the north gate and grilled the guard about why he had changed the boy's ID. The guard pointed to the instruction and explained himself. Rules were rules and the ID said the boy was a mime.

Of course, when King Henry recognized his own mistake, his mood only worsened.

King Henry launched into a six-hour tirade and then insisted on three sweeping changes:

1. All IF statements would put the constant value before the variable (e.g., 0 = = Class ID), so that no assignments could happen by mistake;

2. Every new set of rules had to be reviewed by at least one other person for correctness (which, though a great practice in its own right, was instituted because the king wanted someone else to blame for mistakes); and

3. All new rules would be unit-tested by a group of Shakespearean actors. To make time in their schedule, they would cancel all future productions of Macbeth.

Despite the significant overhead of these new regulations,

instituting them saved time in the long run, and the castle launched into an unprecedented period of smooth operation. Even the castle stables, which had two-hundred-page rulebooks, went a full week without any mistakes.

❦

As he recalled the tale, King Fredrick could almost hear his father's voice ask, "What do we learn from this story?"

"Even the best kings can make mistakes when creating rules, but good design and implementation practices can help avoid them," Fredrick whispered to himself.

For a moment he forgot about the castle and the failed spell. The king smiled widely and stared off into space, losing himself in the memories of his childhood.

A hundred feet away, at the north gate, two guards smiled awkwardly back and wondered what to do next. They valiantly held their expressions until the king collected his thoughts and continued with his walk.

Overcommenting

"As you sort the books, it's important to first separate them by floor," Peter explained. "Putting each floor's books on a different shelf of the cart helps to speed up sorting."

From her table in the corner of the masonry section, Shelly heard Gibson sigh. She glanced over at the pair of apprentice librarians. Peter looked intense as he explained the details of reshelving books. Gibson, who had just started his third day as an apprentice at the library, looked bored.

"I know," Gibson assured Peter.

"This book goes on the third floor, so I'm putting it on the third floor's shelf."

"I understand the concept," said Gibson.

"And this book goes on the second floor, so I'm putting it on the shelf for the second floor. And here's another one for the second floor, so we can put it on the same shelf."

"I get it," interrupted Gibson. "I really do."

Peter looked him over before nodding and waving the junior apprentice on his way. He shook his head as he walked over to Shelly's table.

"What's that all about?" asked Shelly.

"It's this new apprentice, Gibson," said Peter. "I don't think he has the right attitude."

"He seems to be doing well enough," said Shelly.

"Sure. His work is fine. But he's always sighing and rolling his eyes when I explain things to him. He acts as though he already knows it all."

"He probably does," said Shelly. "I heard you explain the part about different shelves to him twice this morning."

"It's important," insisted Peter. "Separating the books by floor can save at least five minutes on a busy day."

Shelly looked at him skeptically. "Is it really *that* important?" she asked. "Important enough to tell him three times in two hours?"

"When I was a new apprentice, I wanted to learn everything—" argued Peter.

"You're boring him," interrupted Shelly. "Worse, you're over-commenting him to death."

"Overcommenting?" asked Peter.

"Yes," said Shelly. "I can tell from here. You narrate every task and every tiny detail. I even heard you tell him how many times to try to light a candle before using a different match."

"After six tries—" started Peter.

"Boring," interrupted Shelly. "That's an unnecessary detail. If anything, these descriptions are probably making it harder to learn. Not only are these super-detailed descriptions annoying, but they also make it hard to follow what's going on. You narrate at such a low level that it's difficult to understand what you're actually describing.

"Take the candles," suggested Shelly. "I bet you could sum the entire process up in one sentence: 'Check the candles and relight any that have gone out.' Go on. Try it."

Peter looked back blankly.

"Say it," urged Shelly.

"Detailed comments help," responded Peter defiantly.

"Too many comments confuse and annoy," argued Shelly. "Marcus once used the Curse of Excessive Commenting on an arrogant blacksmith. He didn't use that spell to be nice."

"He did? Why?" asked Peter.

"It's a long story involving a candle, sleep deprivation, and an argument over teaching skills," said Shelly. "The blacksmith deserved it. In fact, I think Marcus let him off too easy. But that's not important.

"The point is: as much as the curse annoyed Drex, his apprentice Rachel suffered more. The Curse of Excessive Commenting is designed to annoy both the teacher and the student. Commenting on every little action makes it harder to understand what's going on, not easier."

Peter hesitated. "You really think I'm commenting too much? I just want to explain what I'm doing so that he understands."

"Peter, you said 'I am stamping this book as returned' *every* time you stamped a book. That's over two hundred times today! I think he got the concept after the third time."

Peter winced. "You might have a point," he agreed. "Maybe I only need to remind him what to do every fifth or sixth time?"

Shelly groaned. "One good comment at the beginning can explain a whole lot," she assured him.

Peter nodded in agreement but looked unconvinced. As he shuffled back toward the main desk, Shelly couldn't help but feel sorry for Gibson.

Understanding Hidden Costs

"A ND HOW IS YOUR investigation going?" asked the steward.

Marcus had been expecting the question. Why else would the steward invite him to the castle? Now came the unpleasant part. He set his teacup back down on the table and took a deep breath.

"I am afraid that it isn't going well," he said.

"No progress?" asked the steward. "It has been sixteen days since you said that the castle had 'about a month,' which does not leave us with much time. The castle could collapse in a few weeks."

"I'm afraid Hannaldous didn't leave much in the way of documentation," explained Marcus. "The notes he did take are incomprehensible. The spell itself is poorly designed, poorly written, and completely lacking in even the most basic elements of style. I've seen better spells scribbled on bathroom stalls."

The steward pursed his lips but otherwise remained impassive.

"He also appears to have no understanding of his own spell," added Marcus.

"How so?" asked the steward.

"Take underlying costs," said Marcus. "Every data structure or operation you use has some cost. It's every wizard's duty to understand enough about these costs to design efficient spells. Hannaldous didn't have the faintest idea."

"I am not sure that I follow," said the steward. His eyebrows had now furrowed, joining his lips to form an expression of mild unhappiness.

Marcus racked his brain for an analogy the steward could

handle. "Consider accounting," he offered. "You write down entries in a ledger. You fill long tables with amounts to be added or subtracted. You understand how a ledger works, right?"

"I do," said the steward, puffing out his chest. "And I would expect the same of any capable steward. Basic accounting is one of the eight core courses at school."

"Excellent," said Marcus. "Now imagine I gave you a ledger with ten thousand entries, sorted by date."

"A small ledger by castle standards," said the steward.

Marcus smiled. "I'm sure it is. But what if I asked you to insert a new entry before row one hundred?"

Marcus was surprised by how white the steward's face became. He appeared to be hyperventilating.

"That …. That …" the steward mumbled.

"Yes. That would require shifting down nine thousand, nine hundred entries," Marcus said.

The steward nodded.

"You know that because you understand the cost of working with ledgers," said Marcus. "In spells, arrays and strings behave much like ledgers; insertion looks simple but can be expensive.

"It's the same with a simple 'copy' operation. People assume that copying a string is the same as moving a piece of parchment around. But it can be as expensive as copying everything in the string. Imagine someone thinking that copying a ledger would take only a few seconds."

"Do wizards really make that mistake?" the steward asked.

"More often than anyone would like to admit," said Marcus. "It's easy to use some data structure or function in your spell without thinking about it. Most of the time it's fine. But sometimes the costs are extreme."

"And in Hannaldous's spell?"

"Let's just say that Hannaldous didn't have a grasp of any of the hidden costs."

"And was that the problem with the spell?" asked the steward.

Marcus retrieved his teacup and took a sip. "Unfortunately, it wasn't. All these costs do is highlight Hannaldous's lack of skill. The resulting spell is inefficient, but that alone isn't enough to cause this damage."

"I see," said the steward. His eyes finally joined his mouth and eyebrows in expressing his displeasure. It was almost a full expression now. After a moment, he continued.

"I suppose we should move on to the subject of today's visit," he said.

Marcus almost dropped his teacup in surprise. He had no idea what the steward wanted to discuss, and it worried him that this dismal conversation may have been pleasant chit-chat before the real topic.

"Which is?" asked Marcus.

"You brought a guest to the castle recently," said the steward.

"I did?"

"A wizard who speaks to worms," supplied the steward. "I am told she was once quite talented."

"Agatha?" said Marcus. "You want to talk about Agatha?"

"Yes," replied the steward. "I understand that in this case her skills were quite necessary. However, in the future, I must inform you that she is not permitted to practice her arts on the castle's grounds. There is an official edict."

"What?" asked Marcus, stunned.

"If Agatha visits the castle again, she is not allowed to speak to worms," said the steward. He enunciated each word carefully, as though he were speaking to a child.

"Why not?" asked Marcus, his voice rising. "Agatha is a talented wizard and her skills have been vital to this investigation."

The steward held up his hands in a conciliatory gesture. He waited a moment before continuing.

"We do understand her importance to the recent investigation, and we are letting this incident slip. However, Agatha poses a security threat to the kingdom. Much official business is discussed in the courtyards, as well as different flavors of gossip. It would be unfortunate if that information were to leave the castle walls."

"Are you implying that she's a spy?" asked Marcus.

"No," answered the steward. "I am not implying anything. I have no reason to distrust her. The fact is that I am told that worms are surprisingly keen observers, and she speaks to worms. Her skills present a possible security threat."

The steward flashed an overly pleasant smile. He continued, "It is the same logic behind the edict that prevents wizards from leaving anything in the castle. We know listening spells exist, so we eliminate that possibility."

Marcus shook his head in disbelief. "So if she visits the castle, she can't speak with any worms. Correct?"

"Correct."

Marcus shrugged. "Sure. Why not? I'll pass along the message the next time I see her. No chatting up the castle worms." It was a sentence Marcus never would have expected to use.

"Thank you," said the steward with a forced smile. "Now, please do not let me keep you from your work. I believe you have a castle to save."

White Space

F ROM BEHIND THE COUNTER, Peter watched Shelly write furiously. Despite being on vacation, she had been working in the library every day. Each day seemed more intense than the last.

"What is that?" asked Peter as he walked over to check on her.

Shelly looked up from the scroll, eyes glazed. Peter instantly recognized the mental fog that came from being in the zone. Library patrons would get so engrossed in their work that the outside world would effectively cease to exist. Disturbing them always made for an awkward experience, oftentimes requiring the aid of a small air horn.

Shelly seemed to be handling the interruption reasonably well. At least she had responded with more than a grunt.

"Another spell to protect the scrolls?" asked Peter, determined to force Shelly to take even a short rest.

"An analysis spell," said Shelly, her eyes drifting back to the parchment as though being drawn toward it.

"Analyzing what?" asked Peter.

"Rocks."

"The castle problem?" asked Peter. Since she had come back to town, Shelly had had three topics of conversation: the fact that she was stuck learning the basics, how unfair Marcus was, and The Castle Spell.

Shelly nodded. Her eyes were now fixed firmly on the scroll and her lips moved as she read over her work.

Peter looked down at the scroll, trying to see what was so fascinating. It looked like a few dozen lines of neatly printed text.

"What's with all the spaces?" asked Peter.

"Spaces?" echoed Shelly without really hearing the question.

"At the start of lines, mostly," explained Peter. "Some lines are indented. And there's weird spacing in the lines too." He pointed to a few places on the scroll.

This topic seemed to snap Shelly out of her fog. "Oh, those," she said, excitement returning to her voice. "That's white space. It makes the spell more readable."

"Extra spaces make things more readable?" asked Peter. "They make it look funny."

"The spaces denote structure. For example, we indent lines to help represent different blocks of instructions. We also put spaces after colons or around equals signs. It all helps provide visual cues.

"For example, I indent the block of instructions inside a WHILE loop by two spaces."

Shelly pointed to a block of the spell. Then she added underscores in each of the blank spaces to illustrate.

```
WHILE (the ambient magic field is less than X):
__power = power + 10
__ConstructAmbientMagicField(power)
END-WHILE
compute feldsparIndex
```

"The indentation makes it clear that both commands are inside the loop," she finished.

"It wastes parchment. You would shorten it a lot if you took out some of the unnecessary space." As a librarian, Peter naturally worried about the amount of space each scroll took. He chafed at the blatant excess.

"It really does help," responded Shelly adamantly.

"You could at least combine short lines," suggested Peter.

Shelly gasped. "Are you insane? Putting different instructions on their own lines is one of the easiest ways to make spells readable. Sure, there are exceptions. But there's a reason we don't write spells in paragraph form."

Peter stepped back. He hadn't expected such an extreme reaction, even from someone coming out of a work haze.

"Which is?" Peter asked. He was genuinely curious, but quickly realized his question sounded like a challenge.

"Readability!" Shelly said. "Can you imagine a spell that looked like this?"

She scribbled furiously on her parchment:

```
counter=0;WHILE(counter<10):StirPotionClockwise;counter
=counter+1;END-WHILE;counter=0;WHILE(counter<10):Stir
PotionCounterClockwise;counter=counter+1;END-WHILE;
```

She continued, "And all that does is stir a potion 20 times—10 times clockwise, then 10 times counterclockwise. It's not very readable, is it?

"Breaking instructions onto separate lines makes the spell easier to read. Think about instructions in a cookbook. Cooks even number their steps. Step 1, boil the chicken. Step 2, add apricots. Step 3, do something with garlic." Shelly rarely cooked.

"I'm not arguing," tried Peter.

But it was too late; Shelly was off on a tirade. "If Hannaldous had used white space, Marcus would have figured out the spell a long time ago. But Hannaldous had no sense of readability. He didn't even leave spaces around his equals signs. He just squished everything together like people on a bus to the East Alexandria soccer game—packed in without room to breathe."

"Hey now," Peter warned. "Say what you want about cookbooks, but don't take it out on soccer."

"It's all Hannaldous's fault," spat Shelly.

Peter paused, utterly confused. "What is?" he asked.

"That stupid spell," said Shelly. "Everything is a mess. Marcus is always distracted and cranky. The town is in danger. And I have nothing to do."

Peter looked back down at the scroll. "Then why don't you help Marcus?"

"He doesn't need my help," Shelly said. "He's a powerful wizard. Anyway, he already has his hands full."

Peter looked down at the parchments covering the desk.

"It sure sounds like he could use some help. I thought you said he was stuck," Peter pressed on. "And isn't that what you've been working on all week?"

"I haven't been doing anything important—just fiddling with the problem," said Shelly. "And if Marcus wanted help, he would've asked."

Peter shrugged. "Maybe he wanted to shield you from the annoyance or something."

"But the spell is a mess," said Shelly.

"All the more reason to help. Didn't you just say you wanted harder problems? You can't complain about work being too easy and then hide from the hard problems. Deciphering the scroll sounds pretty hard to me. You could learn a lot."

Shelly stared at Peter for a long moment. He could see her brain working, playing out different scenarios.

Without warning Shelly stood up, knocking her chair to the ground. The clatter reverberated through the quiet library. Peter winced and stifled the urge to scold her. Loud noises were not acceptable in the library.

"I have to go," said Shelly.

She swept her work off the table and into a small bag. One pen missed the bag and skittered across the floor. Shelly ignored it.

Seven seconds later, she was running out of the library.

Named Constants

"**N**O MAGIC NUMBERS," MARCUS repeated.

Shelly was well aware of the absurdity of this statement, but she remained focused on the core argument.

"It's not a magic number," said Shelly. "It's just a value—a constant value. The spell requires the potion to be heated to 130 degrees. I wrote 'While the potion is not at 130 degrees: continue to heat and stir.' What's wrong with that?"

Despite the argument—the tenth in two days—Shelly was glad to be back. She had thrown herself into her work, doing everything in her power to help Marcus. In turn, Marcus had piled on the work, loading Shelly with a vast number of castle-related assignments. And, with less than two weeks remaining before the castle's demise, Marcus had an excess of such tasks. The work wasn't glamorous but, for once, Shelly felt useful.

"Magic numbers make the spell harder to read," said Marcus. "You use that same temperature throughout the spell, but always refer to it by number. I'm more concerned about the line three pages down: 'If the sulfur is not at 130 degrees: discard.' It only makes sense if you associate it with the temperature of the potion. It's confusing.

"Remember Hannaldous's instruction: Add the mercury to the bowl containing 10.11 milliliters of water? I had to reread ten pages before I realized he meant the mixing bowl with 10.12 milliliters of water in it. It was a simple error on his part, but I wasted an hour. And what if there had been another bowl containing 10.11 milliliters of water? Something might have exploded."

Shelly groaned. She hated any lesson comparing her work to Hannaldous's spell. Unfortunately, the botched castle spell had become Marcus's standard reference point. He rated everything as either better or worse than the spell. This morning he had described an overcooked omelet as "unworthy of being included in Hannaldous's cookbook."

"What should I do instead?" asked Shelly.

"Use a named constant," suggested Marcus. "Something more meaningful than just 130 degrees, like 'kFinalPotionTemperature.' Define it once at the top of the function. Then you can always refer to it with a meaningful name."

"Why start it with a k?"

"It's an old convention. The k indicates that you're referring to a constant value and not a variable," explained Marcus. He shrugged. "Honestly, I'm not sure where it comes from, but it's nice for consistency. I first saw it in a spell for making clouds form circles; the author used kPi = 3.14159265359."

Shelly could see the logic in using the named constant, but she still bristled at the comparison to Hannaldous. "It seems silly to hide the number behind a constant," she said.

"It has advantages," responded Marcus. "In addition to readability, it makes it easier to change the value. If you later decide the optimal potion temperature is 131 degrees, you will only have to change it in one place. And, of course, if you are repeatedly using a number with many digits, named constants help prevent transcription errors."

"So I replace all numbers in the spell with named constants?"

"Certainly not. It's a judgement call. You use named constants when it makes the spell more readable. For example, it would be absurd to say 'Add kOne teaspoon of water to the bowl' when you could say 'Add one teaspoon.' Not every constant should be named. You have to find the cases where it helps; otherwise it can make the spell more difficult to understand."

Shelly continued to look at her scroll while she racked her brain for another argument.

"If Hannaldous had used named constants for—" began Marcus.

Shelly groaned.

Refactoring

SHELLY SCRATCHED OUT A line from her spell and scribbled a correction in the margin. Scrawled notes covered the scroll. The messy parchment's resemblance to Hannaldous's scroll bothered her, but she comforted herself in the knowledge that this was still a work in progress. The final version would be clean and readable. It would even have comments.

"You need to throw it out and start again," said Marcus.

She jumped at the sudden sound of his voice behind her.

"What?" she said, turning in her chair. "I'll clean it up when I'm done. It won't actually look like this."

"Not the scroll," Marcus said, waving dismissively at the embarrassing tangle of letters. "I meant the spell. You need to throw out the spell and start again."

A wave of anger shot through Shelly. "What?" she asked again.

"The design is wrong," Marcus said.

"You wrote the spell in the first place," said Shelly. "I'm just modifying it to include spiderwebs. Your spell only handled dust, dust bunnies, and dust balls of two inches or less."

"I know," Marcus responded calmly.

"You told me to add spiderwebs to your spell," Shelly continued. "And I'm adding spiderwebs to your spell." The logic remained sound to her as she repeated it.

Marcus took in a deep breath, the type he always took before beginning a lecture. Shelly clenched her fists under the table.

"The spell wasn't designed to handle spiderwebs," Marcus said.

Before Shelly could once again repeat his instructions about adding spiderwebs, Marcus held up his hand. He continued, "You need to refactor the spell."

"Refactor?" asked Shelly.

"Restructure, if you prefer," said Marcus. "You can't force the new behavior into the old spell without making a royal mess of the whole thing. Your function already has ten new arguments and it isn't done yet. And there must be at least twenty-three IF statements on that parchment! Oh my!"

"Refactoring means restructuring the spell without changing the visible behavior. Sure, the internals might change, but the external behavior should remain constant. Refactoring allows you to change the design.

"In this case, you need to first refactor the spell into two new functions. You can put the dust-related behaviors in a new function, CheckForDust, and move air computations into a new function, ComputeAirFlow(object). The behavior will be the same, but you can then add in a new spiderweb-related function here." As he spoke Marcus pointed to various places on the scroll.

"You want me to change the structure of your spell?" Shelly asked.

"Yes," said Marcus. "It makes the final spell cleaner."

"But the original design—"

"The original design served its purpose well enough. But the extended spell needs a new design. One of the easiest ways to mess up a good spell is to keep patching over an insufficient design. The spell becomes a spaghetti of special cases and unnecessary data. Oftentimes it's better to refactor and clean up the design."

"You don't mind?" asked Shelly.

Marcus laughed. "One of the most difficult lessons for a new wizard to learn is not to get too emotionally attached to their work. You can have pride in your work, of course. You *should* have pride in your work. But that shouldn't prevent you from allowing others to make changes or suggest improvements.

"Or even use other wizards' established libraries," Marcus added. "Unfortunately, the same stubborn pride can lead wizards to discount the value of good spell libraries. Master wizards spend years putting together libraries—collections of subspells. If designed well, these libraries are valuable tools and can save countless hours. Yet again and again junior wizards insist on re-implementing the same work." He shook his head.

Shelly stared at the parchment in silence. The thought of refactoring Marcus's spell scared her. Who was she to 'improve' upon Marcus's design?

As though reading her mind, Marcus assured her, "Don't worry. You won't actually be trying to *improve* my design. Requirements change, and sometimes refactoring is necessary. In this case you're refactoring to ensure that you don't mess up a good spell."

Shelly felt her face flush but nodded silently.

Happy with his contribution, Marcus returned to his own work.

Shelly stared at the parchment for another minute. Then she took a deep breath, crumpled up the parchment, and drew a blank sheet from a nearby pile. It was time to start refactoring.

Proximity in Code

Shelly's heart sank as she rounded the corner. Breadista and Ivan stood at the door of Marcus's workshop. Marcus stood opposite them, listening to Breadista. From Breadista's animated gestures and angry expression, Shelly could guess the topic—Ivan's muffins.

Shelly waited around the corner for the visitors to leave. Hiding behind the cheese shop felt cowardly, but she couldn't stomach the prospect of confronting them. The cheese shop's owner gave her a few strange looks through the window, but he didn't say anything. He had come to expect odd behavior from wizards, and besides, she was a loyal patron.

After an agonizing five minutes, Ivan and Breadista left. Shelly walked across the street, ready to face her fate.

The bell over the door cheerfully announced her arrival with a curt "Hello." Shelly had never understood why Marcus had given the bell a Scottish accent, but it had never bothered her until now. Today, though, she felt betrayed by the bell's greeting.

Marcus waited in a chair.

"Hiding behind a cheese shop seems a little childish," he said. "I expect that you saw our visitors and didn't want to join the discussion. Is that correct?"

Shelly said nothing. She stared at a spot on the floor.

"Tell me what happened," Marcus said.

"They didn't tell you?" she asked.

"Of course they did. Now I want your version."

Shelly took a deep breath and jumped in, "I cursed Ivan's muffins."

"Why?" Marcus prompted. His voice sounded calm, which made her more nervous.

"It was a stupid fight. He said that wizards' apprentices never get to learn anything interesting. He called me a mold collector, as though that's all I do."

"And you cursed his muffins for that?"

"I guess."

"You guess that you cursed his muffins? Or you guess that that was the reason?"

Shelly could feel Marcus's stare without looking. She wondered if there was a magic stare for making people feel guilty—something known only to wizards and parents. She shifted about, punctuating the silence with a loud squeak of the floorboards.

"I guess that's the reason," answered Shelly. "I'm certain I cursed the muffins."

"And the wedding cake had nothing to do with it?" confirmed Marcus.

Shelly winced. She couldn't believe Ivan had brought up the wedding cake. What a braggart.

"Cake?" tried Shelly, attempting to sound innocent. She wasn't good at it and failed miserably.

"Breadista said that it's the finest cake he has ever seen an apprentice make," Marcus noted. "Eight layers, perfect flowers, and a working chocolate waterfall. I think Ivan described it as 'epic.'"

"Okay. I might have also been a little jealous of the wedding cake," she answered. "It isn't fair. After years, I'm still learning basic spells and collecting mold. Ivan is making epic cakes and preparing to break the world record for largest muffin tower."

Marcus sighed. "Do you know why you're still learning the basics?" he asked.

"You don't trust me," answered Shelly before she thought better of it. She immediately clapped both her hands to her mouth and shook her head. "I'm sorry. I didn't mean that," she mumbled through her hands. She could feel her face burning with embarrassment.

"It has nothing to do with trust," Marcus explained, his voice still calm. "It's all about knowledge. You see, magic is hard. You have to build up to interesting spells. A baker's apprentice can afford to produce a terrible loaf of bread. A wizard's apprentice can't afford to make a mistake with anything that could explode, turn poisonous, create noxious gases, summon anything evil, or— well—there are a lot of bad mistakes we can make."

"Like causing a castle to crumble," suggested Shelly.

"Exactly," Marcus said with a tight smile. "If Hannaldous had bothered to learn the basics of writing good spells, we wouldn't be in this mess. But, of course, you know that.

"Now that I know why, tell me *how* you did it," said Marcus. His face resumed its serious expression.

"Ivan was making nut oat muffins," answered Shelly. "I turned the nuts into garlic."

A brief smile crept over Marcus's face. He quickly banished it, looking angrier as a result.

"That transformation takes a while. At least three minutes. Ivan didn't notice? What happened when he chopped them up?" he asked.

"I changed them after he chopped them," said Shelly.

"I'm not sure I understand. You'd better tell me exactly what happened."

"You know how you always say: Don't leave things sitting around before using them? You always encourage me to cast the subspells right before I need them and to declare variables near their first use. It keeps things from getting forgotten. Right?"

Marcus nodded. He strongly believed in using proximity to improve understandability. He advocated listing ingredients in groups (one group for each potion), putting similar subspells close to each other in the spell, and declaring variables near their first use. While none of these were unbreakable rules, it was a good practice not to unnecessarily spread context out within a spell.

The importance of proximity had been further reinforced by

Hannaldous's spell. Hannaldous seemed to insist on setting variables at least fifteen pages before they were used. By the time the spell used the variable, Marcus couldn't remember what it stored.

"Well, bakers work differently," said Shelly. "They do a lot of prep work up front, which makes sense for them. To keep track of everything, they use spatial proximity and leave prepared ingredients on their work tables. However, it allows for unnoticed changes." Shelly trailed off, letting the implication hang in the air.

"Such as having the chopped nuts transform into chopped garlic?"

"In my defense, he didn't check," added Shelly. "Every good cook should validate input, right?"

"His mistakes aren't justification," Marcus said. "I'm disappointed. You could have destroyed Breadista's reputation. What if he had sold those muffins?"

"Oh, no," Shelly replied hastily. "It wasn't like that. I wouldn't do that. The muffins weren't for sale. Ivan made them for his girlfriend."

Marcus let out a choked sound that he could have claimed was a cough, but it quickly escalated into an undeniable laugh. He pulled himself together quickly, adding a fake cough in a poor attempt at a cover-up.

"I can see why it took Ivan so long to tell Breadista," said Marcus. He paused for a moment to reflect. When he spoke again, his light tone was gone. "Regardless, your actions were wrong and you must make amends."

Shelly dropped her eyes to the floor, dreading the lecture and whatever punishment was to come.

"I know," she mumbled.

"You will spend the next five days at the bakery, helping Breadista and Ivan. It won't be glamorous work like it is here. I expect you'll be put to work scrubbing bowls and scraping mold out of the corners."

Shelly gasped. "But the castle," she protested. "If I'm working for Breadista, I won't be able to help here. There isn't much time left."

"I'll have to handle it alone for another few days," said Marcus.

The words hit Shelly hard. The guilt from her vacation flooded back, forming a miserable stew with her current guilt over the muffins.

"But—" Shelly started.

"It has been decided. You start at 4 a.m. tomorrow," said Marcus. "Now, I must get back to my own work."

And with those final words, he stood and walked back to his desk.

Comments Revisited

S HELLY HATED HER WORK at Breadista's bakery. Her first three days at the bakery consisted of mopping, scrubbing, and, in one horrific case, attacking the outhouse with a scrub brush and six buckets of soapy water. All the while, she worried about the castle and the counterspell.

To make matters worse, Ivan refused to speak to her. Shelly would be the first to admit that she deserved it. After the muffin incident, Ivan's girlfriend had almost broken up with him. She had unknowingly given the muffins to her great-grandmother, who had been complaining about the lingering smell ever since.

On the fourth day of her servitude, Shelly decided to break the silence. She waited until Breadista stepped out and she was alone with Ivan.

"So how many types of muffins do you make here, anyway?" she asked.

Ivan paused, thinking about the question. Then he walked to a nearby bookshelf and extracted a leather-bound book. It was nearly a foot thick, exceeding the size of even Lawson's Manual of Plant Spells by a good inch. Ivan thumped the book down on the counter, sending up a large cloud of flour. He flipped to the table of contents and ran his finger down the entries, counting.

Two minutes later, he looked up. "One hundred fifty-five," he answered.

"Seriously?" asked Shelly. She would have guessed at most two dozen.

"Most of them are for special occasions," explained Ivan. "Like the pickled herring corn muffins. We only make those around Lord Slevitane's birthday."

Shelly noticed a tiny bit of warmth creep into Ivan's expression—a crack in the iciness.

"What's your favorite?" she asked.

Ivan flipped the pages. "This one," he said. "Breadista's famous eight-chili strawberry muffins. He developed this recipe while he was working in the castle."

Shelly glanced over the page.

Step 5: Cut the strawberries into cubes of 1 cm per side. [This size allows the flavors to blend while preserving the fruit's texture.]
Step 6: Add the strawberries to the dough.
Step 7: Gently stir until the strawberries are mixed into the dough.

"What are the instructions in brackets?" asked Shelly, pointing at the symbols "[" and "]."

"Those are comments," explained Ivan.

"Oh. Marcus is always telling me to comment my spells," said Shelly. "I used to think it was a waste of time."

"I used to think that way too," admitted Ivan. "But comments really are useful. Check out this recipe for strawberry-beet pancakes." He ran to the shelf and extracted a second book. He flipped to a recipe toward the back.

Step 1: Add the salt, sugar, eggs, barley, strawberries, mashed beets, and oil to the bowl in exactly that order, stirring exactly three times between each ingredient.

"See?" prompted Ivan.

"No," admitted Shelly.

"The instruction tells you what to do, right?" said Ivan.

"Yes," agreed Shelly.

"And you could follow it?"

"Sure."

"But what if you wanted to make *lemon*-strawberry pancakes? How would you change it?"

"I don't know."

"Exactly!" cried Ivan. "Because this recipe provides no context. It doesn't tell you *why* you need to add things in a certain order."

Shelly looked back at Ivan. "It does tell you what to do, though," she ventured. "So it isn't terrible. If you want to follow that exact recipe, you can."

"But it doesn't give you any explanation of what the recipe is actually doing. It gives you a list of instructions and assumes that you know enough about strawberry-beet pancakes to follow along. Comments would answer the 'why?'"

"So you like writing comments?" Shelly asked. Although she accepted their value, Shelly had never found writing comments enjoyable.

"I do now," Ivan admitted.

"Even if you're the only one using the recipe?" asked Shelly.

"Especially then," said Ivan. "Breadista would always tell me: 'Just because it's obvious to you at this moment doesn't mean you won't forget it.'

"Of course, I didn't believe him until I had to reread an old recipe of mine. I had written it six months before and couldn't remember why I had used bacon. It took me ten hours to remember. You can be certain I added a comment after that."

"That's it?" asked Shelly. "You became a fan after forgetting the logic behind a single recipe?"

Ivan laughed. "Years ago, Breadtista found the perfect way to reinforce the importance of good comments. It happened back when he was working at the castle, before he opened his own shop. Legend says that he was tutoring Princess Ann at the time and she refused to write comments. To prove his point, he made her work from the worst notes of previous students.

"Now he does that with all his apprentices. I find it agonizing. Sometimes I have no idea what the instructions mean. Other times, they go on forever."

Ivan flipped a few pages back in the second book. "Look at this this one:"

Step 1: Measure out a quarter of an ounce of yeast into a small bowl. [We put it into a bowl so that we can add water in step 2 to activate the yeast.]

Step 2: Add two tablespoons of warm water to the bowl with the yeast. [We add the water to the bowl in order to activate the yeast.]

Step 3: Wait five minutes. [We wait five minutes in order to allow the yeast to activate in the water.]

"It's painful," said Ivan. "I think someone even spilled water on it in order to spare anyone else from reading it." Ivan pointed to the smudged letters and water stains. "Too bad they failed. It's still legible enough for Breadista to use as an example."

"Maybe you should spill something darker on it, like coffee," Shelly offered.

Ivan chuckled. "I thought about squishing some blueberries on the page."

"Veronica would have a fit if she heard you talk about wasting blueberries!"

"Yeah," Ivan agreed solemnly. "I wouldn't want to face her wrath."

They stood in silence, each imagining a different variation of blueberry-inspired rage. Shelly shuddered.

"I've seen some amazingly bad examples too," offered Shelly. "I've seen spells that are completely indecipherable."

"Like that spell Marcus is working on?" asked Ivan.

Shelly felt a rush of guilt. "Hannaldous's spell? How did you know about that?"

"I heard Marcus mention it to Breadista while we were visiting the other night. Marcus said it was a mess."

Shelly felt her face flush as she remembered that night and the ignominy of hiding behind the cheese shop.

"What about it?" asked Shelly.

"Is it well commented?" asked Ivan.

Shelly sighed. "Of course not," she said.

"There you go," said Ivan. "Another good example."

Design in Kitchens

THE FINAL DAY OF Shelly's "employment" at Breadista's seemed to drag on forever. The kitchen sparkled—the result of her week-long cleaning. Bored and unable to find any remaining dirt to clean, she wandered over to Ivan's work table. He stood in front of the low wooden table, putting the final decorations on a wedding cake.

"That cake is amazing," she said.

Ivan smiled and blushed. He leaned close to the cake and carefully adjusted a small candy flower.

"The design was the hardest part," he said.

"The pattern?" asked Shelly.

"No," said Ivan, looking up from the cake. "The overall design. The structure of the cake, the plan for constructing it, the details, everything. It all had to be designed first. Otherwise I might have gotten halfway through before realizing that the weight of the flowers made it lean to the left. Instead, I figured that out ahead of time and reinforced the left side with slices of pound cake."

"Really?" said Shelly. "I had no idea so much thought went into a cake."

"You don't know the half of it," said Ivan. He walked to a bookshelf and extracted a battered notebook. He flipped to a random page and placed it on the table in front of Shelly.

The notes could have put a physics textbook to shame. Crude drawings and dense mathematical formulas filled the entire page. Arrows connected the equations to the corresponding parts of the cake.

"You do all this for a cake?" she asked, amazed. The notes and diagrams rivaled Marcus's most complex spells. Shelly marveled at the lifelike smile on the stick figure eating his second helping.

"You have to," insisted Ivan. "You can't improvise. Making a cake is like cooking a five-course meal. You need to plan ahead."

"A five-course meal?" asked Shelly. She knew she had heard that somewhere before.

"My first week here, Breadista told me some true horror stories. He's seen some absolute disasters in the kitchen."

"Like what?" asked Shelly, genuinely curious.

"His favorite story is about his first boss, Chef Pepperton ..."

⚜

"I can fix this," Chef Pepperton said to himself as he rummaged through a box of fresh vegetables. "I just need some radishes."

Behind him, the kitchen was in chaos. The other cooks dashed about, trying to prepare the five-course meal.

"Radishes?" shouted Chef Pepperton. "Do we have any radishes?"

"No," replied another chef.

Pepperton turned back to the box. "I can fix this," he mumbled. "Carrots. I can do it with carrots."

Then he announced, "We are changing the menu to carrot ravioli. Carrot ravioli."

In the back corner of the kitchen, Breadista, the junior dessert chef, groaned. Since Chef Pepperton had now claimed the carrots, Breadista scratched his plans for carrot cake and started working on a chocolate pudding.

"How's the appetizer coming?" Pepperton asked.

"A little burned, but we can peel off the worst bits," answered his assistant.

Pepperton looked at the stovetop. Three pots and two pans occupied the stove's five burners. Delicious aromas crept from two of the pots and a beautiful sauce simmered in one of the pans. In the other pan, the charred tomatoes for the appetizer sent up curly wisps of black smoke. The final pot contained boiling water, although Pepperton couldn't remember why. Most likely, he had meant to boil something.

Pepperton cursed under his breath and surveyed the countertop for inspiration. "Add some lime juice and call it something festive. Make sure it has the word 'burned' in its name."

An hour ago he had felt better about this meal—confident, even. "I can whip up a meal for his majesty," he had boasted. "I'm sure we have everything we need in the kitchen."

"If we do ravioli, we need another burner," noted his assistant. "Something else will have to come off."

Pepperton counted the burners. Even if they took off the now-charring tomatoes, they were one burner short. He scanned the kitchen, again noticing the mysterious pot of boiling water.

"Forget the mashed potatoes," he said, his memory kicking in. "Throw the potatoes in the fire for forty minutes and call them charred potatoes. Say they go with the tomatoes. We'll use the boiling water for the ravioli."

"I need the fire for the salad," protested the assistant.

"Make it a cold salad," ordered Pepperton. "And where's the salt?"

"Over here," called Breadista.

Pepperton dashed over to retrieve the salt.

"And the radishes?" asked Pepperton.

"You switched to carrots," the assistant reminded him.

"Hold on a second," said Pepperton. "I think I might need to write this down."

An unnatural hush fell over the kitchen. The silence was worse than if everyone had screamed what Pepperton knew they must be thinking. He could hear his own boastful words echo through his head: "We don't need any planning. We've done this a hundred times. We'll just put something together." He shook his head to clear away the doubts and tried to concentrate on saving the meal.

He was halfway through writing down a menu when his

assistant interrupted him. "Chef, your carrots are burning."

Pepperton groaned and crossed "Carrot Ravioli" off his menu.

⚜

Shelly smiled as Ivan finished the story. She could only imagine how Marcus would react to such an environment.

"At least it ended well for him, though," said Ivan.

"Pepperton?" asked Shelly.

"No, Breadista," said Ivan. "As Breadista described it, dessert was the highlight of an otherwise terrible meal. The king immediately hired Breadista to work at the castle."

"What happened to Pepperton?" asked Shelly.

"He became a popcorn vendor in New Alexandria," said Ivan. "No need to design popcorn ahead of time. You just heat it until it pops."

Shelly wondered if there was a magical equivalent of making popcorn.

Test-Driven Development

TWENTY-FIVE MINUTES BEFORE CLOSING, Veronica arrived at the bakery. She stood on the other side of the counter, watching Shelly and Ivan carefully.

"Are you two friends again or what?" she asked.

Before either of them could respond, Veronica continued, "More importantly, can I shop here again? I hate getting my muffins from the mall. Their blueberry muffins are grainy. These are the only decent muffins within 3.14 miles."

Ivan smiled. He turned to a basket on the wall, plucked out a fresh blueberry muffin, and handed it to Veronica. "Grainy blueberry muffins are a crime," he said.

Shelly could see him beaming.

"So what were you talking about?" Veronica asked as she peeled off the muffin's baking paper.

"When?" asked Shelly. She hadn't said a word since Veronica arrived.

"When I came in," said Veronica. "It looked like an exciting conversation. Ivan was waving his arms around and everything."

"Oh," said Shelly. "Breadista gave Ivan an impossible task."

"Ten million muffins by tomorrow?" asked Veronica. "Or a muffin the size of a house? Or—"

"A recipe for a picky patron," Ivan said.

"So?" said Veronica, sounding disappointed. "Just make what he likes."

"That's the problem," said Shelly.

"He doesn't want any of his normal orders," moaned Ivan. "He wants something new, and he has more conditions. It has to be at least as moist as a blueberry muffin, be denser than a bran muffin, and taste like cranberry."

"So?" said Veronica.

"We don't have a recipe that can do that," explained Ivan.

"Create one," offered Veronica simply.

"Baking doesn't work that way," said Ivan. "It's a process of discovery."

"Use test-driven development," said Veronica. "It might take a few tries, but you'll get it."

"Huh?" said Ivan.

"Test-driven development?" asked Shelly.

Veronica shrugged. "It's a good technique for some people," she said. "When you design a new approach, you start by creating tests for it. Then you work on the implementation until the tests pass."

Veronica looked at her friends' blank faces.

"Take Shelly's work," she continued. "If she was creating a new spell for collecting mold or something, she would start by creating the test cases needed, like she might test that she can make a piece of mold float toward her. Then Shelly would write the new spell, improving it until all the tests pass.

"The point is, you start with the tests to help focus the actual design. Granted, some people prefer to use a hybrid approach and write tests in parallel or immediately after the implementation, but I prefer writing the tests first.

"You should use test-driven development, Shelly. Remember the time you forgot to test your potions and made yourself vomit for three days?"

"Three hours," Shelly corrected her.

"Whatever," replied Veronica. "You should have tested your potions."

Shelly started to object, but Ivan cut in.

"How would test-driven development help with these muffins?" he asked.

"What are the constraints?" Veronica asked. She reached into her pocket and produced a small, grid-lined notebook.

"Uh …" said Ivan.

"It has to be at least as moist as a blueberry muffin, and it has to be denser than a bran muffin," offered Shelly.

"And taste like cranberry," added Veronica as she listed the constraints on the paper. Each constraint was numbered and written as a test.

1) Muffin moistness greater than or equal to blueberry muffin

2) Muffin density greater than bran muffin

3) Muffin tastes like cranberry

"What else?" she prompted.

"It can't have any apricots, corn, flaxseed, raspberries, honey, or chicken," said Ivan.

Veronica listed six more constraints on the paper.

"Didn't you say something about temperature?" asked Shelly.

"Oh yeah," said Ivan. "The muffins have to taste good when cool. And they need to be at least as grainy as corn muffins."

"And you already said it has to be new," Veronica said as she added another three constraints.

"Um …" Ivan replayed the list in his head. "That's it, I think."

"That gives us twelve tests," said Veronica. "Design a recipe that tries to solve these constraints. When the first batch comes out, run the tests. I'm happy to help with that part. Then see which tests pass and which ones fail. Improve the recipe accordingly."

"Oh," said Ivan. He glanced around a few times as if looking for a recipe that wasn't there. Finding nothing, he scribbled a few notes on a sheet of baking parchment. In under a minute he had produced twenty lines and moved on to measuring ingredients.

"Needs to be dense … no raspberries … and good at room temperature …" Ivan mumbled under his breath as he worked.

Shelly was shocked. Ivan was creating a new recipe with the tests in mind. She glanced over at Veronica, who was staring longingly at the basket of blueberry muffins.

Soon Ivan had filled a tray with muffin dough and shoved it into an oven. He turned back to Veronica.

"How did you hear about this test-driven development?" he asked.

"We use it all the time in accounting," said Veronica.

"You do?" asked Ivan.

"Of course we do," said Veronica. "The field has matured a lot since the early days of cowboy accounting. Our processes have improved and standards have emerged. Last year the final few holdouts even agreed to recognize decimal points."

Ivan cocked his head to the side, but didn't pursue the topic.

After barely ten seconds of silence, Veronica decided to fill the conversational void with a monologue about capital depreciation of stone walls and its relation to the castle's deterioration. Ivan listened politely without retaining any information. Shelly leaned against the counter and didn't even pretend to listen.

They both sighed with relief when the timer rang.

"You promised you would try these," Ivan reminded Veronica as he pulled the muffins from the oven.

As Veronica chewed, she looked down at her list of tests.

"Fails two of the tests," she declared. "It's too smooth—nothing like a corn muffin. And it's not quite as dense as a bran muffin."

"Oh," said Ivan. He turned back to the recipe. His lips moved as he reread it. "I think I made a mistake in the oat computation," he said finally.

He made a correction to the parchment and sprang back into action. The ingredients were measured, mixed, and scooped into a clean muffin tin. He shoved the new batch into the oven.

"Don't worry," said Veronica. "Sometimes it takes a few rounds of testing. But each time, you're fixing some bugs."

"You already made muffins that passed most of the tests," added Shelly.

Ivan nodded. He turned to Veronica. "Thanks," he said. "I would never have thought of this approach on my own."

Veronica smiled widely. "See?" she said. "Even bakers can benefit from testing."

Defensive Programming

"**T**HE FIRST STEP IS to check that the potion doesn't contain any water," explained Marcus.

"It doesn't," answered Shelly without writing anything down. She felt giddy with excitement. Upon her return to Marcus's lab, he had enlisted her help in creating a new stabilizing potion for the castle.

The potion wouldn't fix the problem; it was a temporary patch at best. But after twenty-six days of limited progress, Marcus needed to buy himself time.

Marcus watched her, awaiting a response.

"I made it myself," Shelly added.

"Shelly," Marcus started, his tone weary. "The spell of De-Dustification is finicky. One drop of water in the potion would speed up the castle's demise, which would be bad. In fact, you probably want to use an assert here."

"An assert?" said Shelly.

"It's a magical subspell that will check that a given condition holds. If the condition doesn't hold, for example if the potion contains water, then the assert fails and crashes the whole spell."

"Sounds like overkill," said Shelly.

"It's not overkill," said Marcus. "The consequences of continuing the spell would be extremely dire. And asserts are useful for lesser failures too. Sometimes it's better for a spell to fail fast rather than limp along and try to patch over issues.

"Consider the Spell of Glowing Ants," continued Marcus. "The spell is designed to work on one ant at a time. It can't handle the case where there are zero ants or two ants. So the spell should always begin with an assert that there is exactly one ant.

"Sure, we could patch over the problem of multiple ants by finding the closest ant or choosing one at random, but that introduces unpredictable behavior. It's better to just crash and restart the spell."

"I was very careful about the water," said Shelly.

"I know," Marcus said with great patience. "But think about the long term. What if you give your notes to someone else? What if you buy the potion in the future instead of making it yourself? Or what if you just forget to check? You have to learn to write spells well. It's always better to practice defensive spell creation."

Shelly looked confused. "Like the Shield Spell?"

"That's a defensive spell," answered Marcus. "I mean *creating* spells defensively. Defensive creation is a technique for avoiding disasters within a spell. For example, spells should validate their ingredients before using them. It's like math. Before you divide two numbers, you want to make sure that you aren't dividing by zero."

"That seems inefficient," said Shelly. "Shouldn't we just be careful?"

"It does take extra time," replied Marcus. "But it's worth it. Remember the spell of Persistent Jazz Music?"

Shelly shuddered. "I have no idea how you enjoy that music. It's almost as bad as marching bands."

"Nothing is as bad as marching bands," Marcus declared. "Regardless, do you remember what happened when I tried to cast that spell last month?"

"Elevator music," Shelly said with a small smile.

"Loud elevator music!" cried Marcus. "Thunderous elevator music!" Unlike Shelly, he didn't consider elevator music to be an improvement over jazz.

Shelly stifled back an argument that, regardless of the circumstances, elevator music could never be considered thunderous. At worse, it had been *intense*.

"And that happened because?" prompted Marcus.

"You didn't check the inputs?" guessed Shelly.

"Exactly! I never checked that the first spell, the Spell of Musical Preference, finished correctly. Instead of taking my preferences into account, the spell latched onto *your* preferences. Elevator music! That's why you create spells defensively."

Shelly resisted the urge to laugh as she flashed back to his reaction at the time. She had never heard him scream so loudly.

Instead, she asked, "Is defensive spell creation just validating inputs?"

"No," said Marcus. "Defensive spell creation is a general technique. The goal is to make programs robust against errors or unexpected conditions.

"For example, the Const Spell of Immutability is an example of defensive programming—you mark variables as constant to prevent them from being accidentally modified somewhere else in the spell.

"Or, have you heard the king tell the story about his father and the north gate? Of course you have; anyone who's spent more than six minutes with the king has heard that story, repeatedly. One of King Henry's new rules was to put the constant value before the variable in all IF statements, so that no one made assignments by mistake. Defensive rule creation!

"And then there are error codes and exceptions," started Marcus. Shelly realized that he hadn't even paused to take a breath. "There is an entire field of study on how a subspell should communicate that something went wrong. Some spells return detailed error codes. Other spells use an advanced form of magic called 'throwing exceptions.' If we consider each approach carefully—"

"Okay. I've got it," Shelly interrupted. "Defensive spell creation is a combination of making it harder to make mistakes and making it easier to handle bad situations that do arise."

"Uh, well, yes." said Marcus.

At the top of her parchment, Shelly wrote:

1) Check that the potion does not contain any water.

"Okay," said Marcus, satisfied. "Let's finish this spell and see if we can slow the damage to the castle."

Variable Initialization

THE NEXT DAY, MARCUS and Shelly packed their supplies and headed to the castle. While the spell of De-Dustification wouldn't stop the decay, Marcus hoped that it would at least slow the damage. The spell would bond together the dust particles into a protective film.

When they arrived at the castle, Marcus inspected the damage as he waited for the steward. Long ago he had learned to secure an owner's permission before casting spells on buildings. Castle owners could be particularly uptight about such formalities.

The steward didn't keep them waiting. If anything, he was more impatient to see them than they were to see him.

"Good morning," the steward greeted them. His face indicated that the morning was anything but good. "Any progress on the spell?"

"Some," hedged Marcus. "As I indicated in my pigeon message, we can apply a temporary patch for now. It'll protect the castle and give us a few extra days."

The steward had read the message ten times since its arrival. He knew precisely what Marcus could and couldn't do at this point. Still, he couldn't help but be disappointed.

"Please proceed," the steward said.

"I will require a few additional materials: two empty bowls, six flat stones, a pound of sugar, and a live jazz band."

"A live jazz band?" asked Shelly, her head snapping up. "I don't remember needing that for the spell."

"It's not for the spell," explained Marcus. "I thought it would make the afternoon more pleasant. The spell takes a few hours to set up, so we'll have some time to wait."

The steward seem unperturbed. "I will get the bowls, stones, and sugar presently. I will need to check on the availability of his majesty's jazz band, though. I believe they had a late night last night."

After the steward left, Marcus and Shelly started to prepare the spell. Shelly climbed a short ladder with the first three potions. As Marcus had taught her, Shelly checked each potion carefully for water before applying it to the castle's wall. Marcus hunched over a picnic table, making notes on the current temperature and wind speeds.

When a young man arrived with the requested supplies, Marcus waved him toward the table without looking up. "Put them down there," he said.

Still concentrating on the scroll, Marcus grabbed one of the bowls and pulled it toward him. He looked up long enough to select a bottle of peach-flavored vinegar and uncorked it. "One bottle flavored vinegar," he mumbled to himself.

"Wait!" cried Shelly.

Marcus froze with the bottle half-tipped toward the bowl. He looked up at Shelly, who had jumped down from her ladder and was hurrying toward him.

"There's something in there," explained Shelly. "Something moving."

Marcus's eyes darted to the bowl. Sure enough, a small tree frog stared back at him. It blinked.

"What's this?" asked Marcus.

"A frog," answered the delivery boy.

Marcus looked at him sharply. "I don't need a frog. I needed an empty bowl."

"I thought it was empty," admitted the boy. "It was in a pile of clean, empty bowls, so I assumed ..." He trailed off in embarrassment.

"Ribbit," added the frog.

Marcus scooped out the frog and placed it on the ground.

"The frog would have ruined the spell," he noted.

Shelly beamed. "It's like you taught me. It's always important to make sure your variables, data structures, and bowls are all initialized to the value that you expect before using them. Make sure your bowls are clean and empty, your counters are set correctly, your parchment doesn't have other notes scribbled on it, and so forth."

In truth, it was a tale from Ivan that had driven home the lesson. He had ruined an entire batch of cookies after forgetting to reset the timer, which he had left on the bread setting. Instead of baking the cookies for the necessary ten minutes, Ivan had found charred lumps when the timer rang forty minutes later.

Marcus fell silent for a moment, his face darkening. "I must be getting sloppy. The spell would have been ruined, and the frog traumatized."

Shelly stifled a response and turned back to her own work. Despite his lack of even a "thank you," she knew that she had saved the spell. She would bask in this moment for the rest of the day. However, she was smart enough to do so silently.

Premature Optimization

SOMETHING HAD GONE HORRIBLY wrong. At first, Shelly thought Marcus had had a breakthrough. He sat at his table, furiously scribbling on a roll of parchment. Then she heard the mumbling.

"I know I can make it fast," muttered Marcus for the eighth time, which disturbed Shelly more than the previous seven mumblings. For some reason, eight repetitions seemed to cross the threshold into excessive.

"Is everything okay?" she asked.

"I know I can make it fast," he mumbled without looking up.

"What isn't fast enough?" Shelly asked.

Marcus seemed to perk up at the question. "This subspell. It takes a full minute to cast. I know I can get it down to less than five seconds."

"Why?"

"Because I'm a brilliant wizard!" Marcus snapped.

The ferocity of his tone shocked Shelly. She had heard him yell like that only once before, and that outburst had been directed at sulking roses—not at a person.

"I meant, why does it need to be cast in five seconds? Do you need to cast it before another spell wears off?"

"No."

"Do you have a limited time window due to an eclipse?"

"No."

"Will there be a fire, a troll attack, or something else dangerous happening while you cast it?"

"No. None of that."

Shelly's mind searched for other explanations.

"Then why?" she asked. "A minute doesn't seem like too long."

"It's too long for what this spell does," argued Marcus. "I can make it much faster."

Shelly stood quietly at the end of the table, trying to find a new way to phrase the question. Given what Marcus had developed so far, the spell would already take hours to cast. Why was another minute important? Yet something else bothered her more, something she couldn't place.

"What does the subspell do?" she finally asked.

"The loop is the problem," Marcus mumbled to himself.

"What does the subspell do?" Shelly repeated. "Perhaps I can help."

"It dries out the immediate vapor fields," Marcus responded in an irritated tone. "That's trivial to see."

"I thought …" Shelly trailed off.

She knew what was wrong.

"Hey!" she almost shouted as a thrill of excitement and fear raced through her.

Marcus looked up, his face twisted in annoyance. "If you can't stay quiet long enough for me to work—" he began.

Shelly cut him off. *"Design! Measure! Optimize!"* she shouted, hoping that she remembered the correct order.

"How dare you!" Marcus roared back.

"It's for your own good," she whispered before shouting the words again. *"Design! Measure! Optimize!"* She waved her hands in a quarter arc, a faint blue streak following her motions.

Marcus stood, his face a rigid mask of anger. His chair clattered to the floor. He reached for his staff.

Shelly grabbed a glass of water and splashed the contents on his face. While not necessary for the countercurse, the cold water provided a momentary distraction. Shelly tried not to enjoy his shocked sputtering.

"Design! Measure! Optimize!"

The amusement lasted less than a second. Marcus grabbed his staff.

Fear flooded through her. The words of the spell caught in her throat as she looked at Marcus. She didn't have much time. With great effort, she forced herself to continue.

"I command you to see clearly," Shelly choked out. Her voice was barely above a whisper, but rose with each word. "To understand the cost. *Design! Measure! Optimize!*"

She waved her hand again and a dull red aura seeped from Marcus and dissipated into the air.

A look of shock crossed Marcus's face, and he collapsed back where the chair had been. He landed on the floor with an undignified thump.

"Toad's hairs," he cursed.

Shelly watched him warily. She debated another round of chanting. It wouldn't do to have the countercurse derailed by a simple off-by-one error.

After a moment, Marcus looked up at her. He reached out with his right hand. "Help me up."

Shelly leaned forward and helped pull the wizard to his feet. Marcus dusted himself off, righted the chair, and promptly flopped down into it.

"Toad's warts," he cursed. Shelly flinched at the language.

He sat in silence for a few minutes before looking up at her again.

"Thank you," he said. "How did you know?"

Shelly stifled a smile at her second victory of the week. She knew it wasn't safe to gloat.

"You were obsessed with optimizing a tiny subspell in a part of the spell that you'd already changed ten times. Not only did the subspell not matter, you weren't even done with the design. Odds are that you'll throw out that whole part of the spell tomorrow."

Marcus nodded. "The more I work on this spell, the more I hate Hannaldous."

"Do you think it was a trap?" asked Shelly.

Marcus shook his head. "No. Hannaldous isn't that smart. The Curse of Premature Optimization is easy to weave into a spell by accident. All it requires is too much focus on one aspect. For all I know, I could've done it to myself."

Shelly remained respectfully silent. She had suffered the Curse of Premature Optimization twice herself. The aftereffects included a headache, a dry mouth, and a raging sense of embarrassment.

"Thank you again," Marcus said. He sighed. "This is the tenth time I've had that horrid curse. Each time is more embarrassing than the last. You'd expect at my age that I would be immune— that I would know you shouldn't optimize the low-level details until you've finished the high-level design and measured the actual performance. Otherwise you could just be wasting time.

"At least you got to practice a counterspell, though," he added. "I suppose I should take a break for today and teach you a few more. For all I know, Hannaldous accidentally buried other curses in his work. From the looks of it, I'd expect the Curse of Indecipherable Text, the Curse of Too Many Loops, and the Curse of Excessive Drooling. I'd feel better knowing you were prepared to help in case I run into one of those."

Shelly felt a surge of pride. She nodded eagerly while trying to look reserved and respectful.

Marcus watched her.

"Go on and smile," he said. "You've earned it."

With those words, Shelly's entire face lit up.

Understandable Loops

IVAN STOPPED OUTSIDE THE castle's kitchen and consulted his delivery slip.

"Chef Casserolii?" he called.

"Put them on the table," responded a tall chef near the back of the room. She stood by the ovens, gently resting a hand against the iron doors. Her eyes were closed.

Ivan proceeded to haul ten baskets of dinner rolls into the kitchen and onto the prep table. When he finished, he turned back to Chef Casserolii.

"How bad is the chimney?" he asked. He knew the chimney's collapse must be a sore point for the kitchen staff. Until this morning's collapse and subsequent dinner roll order, Ivan had never heard of the castle outsourcing anything edible.

Chef Casserolii shrugged. "We'll be okay," she said. "The castle has two other functional kitchens. The baking will go on."

Ivan paused. "But you ordered five hundred dinner rolls," he said. "You never order rolls!"

"I had to fire our roll chef," Chef Casserolii explained. "He had been doing a terrible job for weeks."

"Really?" said Ivan. "But rolls are so simple. Was he using the New Atlantian method or the West Arctic method?"

Chef Casserolii raised an eyebrow. "I see you know your roll recipes," she said. "He was using his own method. Take a look."

She retrieved a sheet of parchment from a nearby shelf and handed it to Ivan. Ivan skimmed the recipe until he came to the instructions for kneading dough. He gasped in shock and pointed at the instructions.

```
counter = 0
WHILE (counter < 100):
    IF the dough is stretchy: set the counter to 100
    knead the dough
```

"He used this?" he asked in disbelief. "He actually wrote these instructions?"

"You see the problem then?" she asked.

"It's completely unintelligible," said Ivan. "The counter doesn't actually count anything. It's only modified when the stretchiness condition is met. How could he write a loop like that?

"And even if 'counter' did count out 100 rounds of kneading, changing a loop counter this way is a disaster waiting to happen. What if he changes the recipe to knead 200 times? Then he has to remember to set change the internal IF statement as well."

Chef Casserolii studied Ivan. "How would you fix it?"

"First I would move the stretchiness condition into the WHILE's test itself. The WHILE's condition should be simple and easily understandable. You knead the dough until it feels stretchy."

As he spoke, Ivan removed a small pencil from behind his ear and started scribbling on a nearby piece of baking parchment.

"Actually, I would also keep a counter of the number of iterations," he continued. "Counters can be useful in preventing infinite loops. Once I found an infinite loop in a soup recipe. I stirred the bisque for ten hours before Breadista noticed and yelled at me. I would hate to have anyone knead bread dough for more than an hour."

He handed the parchment to Chef Casserolii.

```
count = 0
WHILE (the dough is not stretchy and count < 100):
    knead the dough
    count = count + 1
```

"I see Breadista has taught you well," said Chef Casserolii. "You keep the loop conditions simple and understandable. You guard against potential infinite loops. And you don't mess with loop counters to terminate a loop early."

Ivan smiled proudly.

"It happens that I'm looking for a new roll chef," Chef Casserolii said. "Interested?"

Ivan felt his heart jump. A job in the castle kitchens was an opportunity of a lifetime.

Yet he hesitated. He wasn't ready to leave Breadista's program. And, although he wouldn't admit it to himself, the thought of giving up muffins to specialize in rolls filled him with a vague sense of dread.

"I'm honored," Ivan replied carefully. "But I want to finish Breadista's program. I still have a lot to learn."

Chef Casserolii gave him a knowing smile. "I understand," she said. "But come back when you're done. We'll see if we can find an opening. We always need someone who can write a decent loop."

Functional Side Effects

TWENTY-NINE DAYS INTO HIS investigation, Marcus had a breakthrough. By this point, the castle's stability could only be called doubtful. Even the castle's pigeons refused to land on the wall, preferring the comparative safety of a nearby rotten oak tree.

"He only uses one function, and he messes it up," exclaimed Marcus.

Shelly, who had been slumped over the table asleep, sat up in surprise. She dabbed at her mouth, checking for drool. "Huh?"

"DoStuff," answered Marcus.

"I'm sorry. I was just so tired," she spluttered.

"No, no, the *function* DoStuff," explained Marcus. "Hannaldous used one function in his entire spell, and he messed it up."

"Really? How?" asked Shelly.

"Undocumented side effects."

"Side effects? You mean the mushrooms?"

"No. *Functional* side effects," explained Marcus. "A side effect is when the function does something to one of its inputs or to the global state. Remember my Spell of Self-Playing Violins?"

"Of course," Shelly replied. "That was the best performance of Sir Mandelbrot's fractal symphony I ever heard."

"A few people actually wept," said Marcus, momentarily basking in the memory. "But remember how the violins' owners reacted after the spell?"

"That wasn't fair," Shelly protested. "All the spell did was tune the violins."

"I never said their reaction was fair," said Marcus. "However, it shouldn't have been a surprise. I promised them that the spell wouldn't change their violins, that it would only move the bows and perform the fingerings. The unusual tuning was a side effect."

"The violins were fine once they had new strings," Shelly said.

"Regardless, hidden or unexpected side effects can be dangerous. At the very least, side effects should be clearly documented," said Marcus.

"For example," continued Marcus, "the Spell of Mirroring has a function that outputs the updates to a sheet of parchment. This interaction had to be clearly documented. If it wasn't, a new user might not expect the parchment to be modified."

Shelly's mind raced back to Hannaldous's scroll. She had read the DoStuff function dozens of times and had never noticed a side effect. She tried to match Marcus's description of side effects with what she remembered about the function.

"What's DoStuff's side effect?" she asked.

Marcus laughed with equal parts amusement and annoyance. "The function overwrote one of the inputs—the mass index, to be precise. Every time Hannaldous used the function, the input mass index was overwritten by the number ten.

"The function overwrites it right at the end, so the function still returns the correct answer. But he overwrote one of the input values in the process. So calling DoStuff with a variable could have unknown consequences for the calling function."

"Overwrote?" asked Shelly.

"Imagine you give me a list of numbers to add," Marcus explained. "I take your list, add the numbers, and give you back the answer, right?"

"Yes," agreed Shelly.

"Now, what if I take the list, add the numbers, erase the fifth number and replace it with the value three, and still return the correct sum of the original list?"

Shelly balked. "Do I need the list for anything else?"

"Exactly," Marcus said. "If you don't use the numbers again then you won't even notice. But, if you do need the original numbers, your data is now wrong.

"That's what DoStuff does. It stomps on an input value and replaces it with the number ten.

"The number ten! Ha! Here he calls DoStuff with the mass of the walls and the value is transformed to ten. So when he tries to use walls' mass in the moisture calculation he uses ten instead. And here he calls DoStuff with the mass of a pebble, and that value is overwritten by ten, too."

"So?" Shelly prompted, not daring to ask the obvious question.

"We can reverse the spell," Marcus answered. "We know what went wrong. We know the current state, thanks to Agatha's worms. And, with a high degree of certainty, we know the weather for the coming week. *We can reverse the spell!*"

Using Mocks for Testing

"How do we test it?" asked Shelly, staring at the eight-page scroll. "We can't just cast it on the castle and hope for the best, right?"

Marcus smiled. "Great question. You're starting to think like a real wizard. How would you test it?"

Shelly thought for a moment. "On a rock," she said.

"Rocks make fine unit tests for some of the subspells, but we need more functionality for the full test. We need to confirm that the windows will still open and that the drawbridge can still be lowered. And we need to test the dynamics. What happens if someone opens a door during the spell?"

"We could find a small abandoned castle," suggested Shelly.

"That would work for a single test. But it's risky. What if the spell doesn't work the first time? We can't go around destroying all the abandoned castles within a day's ride."

Marcus looked at Shelly and waited for the next suggestion.

"Use the debugging spell?" she said.

"Now you're just guessing," Marcus said with a note of irritation in his voice. "The correct answer is that we'll use a mock for testing."

"What's a mock?" asked Shelly.

"A mock castle," explained Marcus. "It has the same interface as a castle and some of the same properties, but it's a fake version that we control. We can control what happens when we open the windows or lower the drawbridge."

"I see," said Shelly. "Where do we get a mock castle?"

"In this case, I think we have to build one. The hardware store stopped carrying them a few years ago. There's not much call for mock castles these days. Too few people respect the value of good testing. In my day, even carpenters would test their ideas on mock castles."

Shelly gasped.

"It was a different time," said Marcus. "Anyway, first up we have to decide what interfaces we need to replicate and what reactions we want to model. Then we'll need six pounds of crushed stone and two barrels of glue."

"Popsicle sticks for the drawbridge," Shelly suggested.

The barest hint of a smile crossed Marcus's face. "Yes," he said. "That would do quite well."

Marcus and Shelly completed the mock castle in under four hours. The resulting creation was somewhere between a grade school art project and a pile of rocks. But style didn't matter, the interface did. The castle had two small glass windows and a tiny operational drawbridge.

As Shelly finished construction, Marcus set to work on a basic spell to dissolve rock. While not as finicky as Hannaldous's curse, it would be sufficient for their tests.

"It seems like a waste," said Shelly, "writing a new spell for testing. You're just going to throw it away later. What good is a spell that only dissolves a castle-shaped pile of stones less than fifteen pounds?"

"We need it for the test," said Marcus. "Sometimes you need to write spells that you know you'll throw away, like a quick prototype or a test condition. While they don't get the same credit as their polished, final spell counterparts, they do have their uses."

"I guess," said Shelly. She returned to the final portion of the assembly, creating a miniature bathroom that drained into the moat. Ensuring the toilets would continue to function was almost as important as saving the castle itself.

Marcus waited for her to finish and then cast his test curse on the mock castle.

"Now the fun begins," he said. He had a twinkle in his eyes that Shelly hadn't seen in a month.

Marcus completed the first three pages of the spell without incident. As he finished each line, Shelly carefully checked the condition of the mock castle. Hope began to build inside her.

On the fourth page, the drawbridge exploded. Wooden shrapnel flew across the room. Marcus tried to shield himself with his notes, but a small splinter embedded itself in his finger.

"Ouch!" he exclaimed. "Toad warts!"

Shelly winced at the language.

"The spell?" she said, not wanting to hear the answer.

Marcus waved dismissively. "The spell's fine. I didn't compensate for the door frame correctly. Stupid arches. It's a simple fix, though. That's why we test."

"But—your language."

"Oh. Sorry about that," said Marcus. "I hate splinters." He began to pick at the tiny sliver of wood in his finger, mumbling under his breath.

Without looking up, he continued, "Can you rebuild the drawbridge while I deal with this wound? I expect we have a few more mock castles to wreck before we get all of the bugs out."

Shelly felt a sudden wave of relief. The spell could still work, and, more importantly, they hadn't discovered the bug by blowing up the *king's* drawbridge.

Rolling Out Changes

THE CASTLE'S ENTIRE STAFF was on hand to observe the deployment of the counterspell. Hundreds of soldiers, pages, cooks, maids, blacksmiths, tailors, and stableboys loitered by the front gate. Of course, it helped that Marcus had insisted on a full evacuation; as a result, most of the staff had nothing else to do.

Shelly noticed that even Agatha had made the trip. She stood toward the back of the crowd with a wheelbarrow full of dirt. Shelly assumed that, given the restrictions against Agatha speaking to the castle's worms, she had instead brought her own worm friends to observe the festivities. It would be dreadfully boring to watch a counterspell without someone to share gossip with.

As they reached the castle, Marcus broke away from the path and strode toward a small group by the refreshment table. There King Fredrick stood with his steward, the captain of the guard, and a few visiting lords. Aside from the steward, the group looked relaxed as they talked and ate muffins.

"I am sorry for the inconvenience," Shelly heard the steward say as they approached. His apology appeared to be directed at the mayor of G'Raph.

"Inconvenient, but necessary," Marcus said as he approached the group. "We've developed a formal rollout plan for this spell. It's imperative that we both minimize risk and maximize control over the castle."

The captain of the guard looked up sharply at the last phrase. His hand shot to the hilt of his sword.

"An unfortunate choice of words," Marcus assured him. "I only meant that we need to prevent any uncontrolled changes. It wouldn't do to have someone slamming doors during the spell. It could throw off the dynamics."

"I am not sure that I understand," said the steward. "Why does it matter if someone is opening or closing doors? Your spell acts only on the material. Is that not correct?"

"Consider the task of rebuilding a bridge," Marcus said. "While the work is going on, you may find it wise to prevent traffic on the bridge. Our spell is much the same. To deploy it safely, we want to prevent anything from changing. We want to shut off the inputs and outputs, so to speak. It will only be for a short while; I assure you that it's all documented in our rollout plan."

"How long will the spell take?" asked the king.

"Nine hours," said Marcus.

"Nine hours?" gasped the steward.

"Yes," confirmed Marcus, "three hours for each time we cast the spell."

"Three times?" gasped the steward.

"Please explain," said the king with a sigh. "What is the actual plan?"

Marcus smiled politely. "Unfortunately, we can't cast the counterspell on the entire castle at once. It would present a race condition."

"Race condition?" asked the steward.

"That is when multiple tasks are running simultaneously and the outcome depends on which one executes first," explained the king. "We had some problems with race conditions in the pigeon network last year. It turned out that the routing algorithms were poorly thought out. We have a new person on it though—one of those scholars from G'Raph of whom my daughter spoke so highly."

G'Raph's mayor beamed.

"King Fredrick is correct," Marcus said. "In this case, the race condition has to do with the weight of the stone. If the spell finishes on the top of the castle before the bottom, the foundations won't be able to take the extra weight."

"So what will you do?" asked the steward.

"A staged rollout, of course," said Marcus. "We'll start by reversing the spell on the foundation. Then we'll reverse the spell on the lower levels, and finally we'll reverse the spell on the upper levels. It'll take three hours for each level, so we'll need nine hours total."

"And the staged rollout will fix the race condition?" said the steward.

"Mostly," said Marcus. "We no longer have to worry about the foundations crumbling, but there will be some extra strain on the points where sections meet. Nothing to be alarmed about, but we have to move fast. We can't let two adjacent sections occupy different states for too long."

"So it is a race against the clock?" asked the steward. Nervousness occupied his entire face, and he was sweating profusely.

"We made sure to provide buffer time between each level," Marcus assured him. "As long as we keep working, we'll have more than enough time."

This reassurance did nothing to satisfy the steward. "Are you sure?" he asked.

"Yes," said Marcus. "That's why we devised a rollout plan for this change. It's a large change to a real castle. We need to be sure of our approach."

"Are you sure about the timing?" insisted the steward.

"Yes," Marcus said. "I triple-checked the calculations."

"And I tripled-checked them as well," Shelly added, prompting a stern look from Marcus.

"And you're confident about the spell itself?" asked the steward.

"Yes," sighed Marcus. "We tested it on a mock castle and Agatha did the spell review."

"I see," said the king before the steward could ask another question. "By all means, please get started."

Marcus gave a short bow and turned toward the castle.

"Now the fun begins," he said to Shelly.

Documentation

MARCUS COMPLETED THE FIRST floor in two hours and forty-seven minutes. He wiped the sweat off his forehead as he finished. Without saying a word, he packed up his magical instruments and proceeded to the next level. Shelly followed him, lugging a heavy folding table.

The process went even smoother on the second level. Two hours and five minutes into the counterspell, Shelly could hear the stone hardening. The walls made a soft grinding sound that sent vibrations through her head. She smiled. The counterspell was going to work. She knew it.

A few minutes later, Marcus sent her ahead to prepare the next area. At this rate, they could be finished before dinner. The prospect sent a flurry of hope through Shelly.

Shelly bounded up the stairs two at a time. She found a quiet room in the center of the castle and went about arranging potions, scrolls, and spare wands. She lit a few candles and confirmed that they provided adequate light. She double-checked each potion label and confirmed that the mixing bowls were empty. Once everything was ready, she skimmed over a spare copy of the counterspell and rechecked everything.

Then she heard the crash.

The sound sent a flood of panic through her and she bolted for the door without thinking. She ran back toward Marcus.

Shelly skidded to a stop inches before a sharp drop. Minutes ago she had walked up a staircase in this very location. Now there was nothing.

She inched her way forward and stared down at the floor

twenty feet below. It was littered with pieces of crumbled staircase.

"Marcus?" she yelled down.

The seconds stretched out as she waited for Marcus to respond. Finally, he poked his head out of a door.

"What happened?" he called.

"The stairs collapsed," Shelly explained. Then for good measure she added, "It wasn't my fault. I was in the other room."

Marcus surveyed the hallways. "This is bad," he stated. "If the stairs are weak enough to collapse on their own, the castle is weaker than I thought. We don't have much time."

"There's another staircase at the far end of the keep," Shelly informed him.

But Marcus shook his head. "The wood is too weak to trust, and we don't have enough time to wait for ladders. You'll have to perform the spell from there."

"Me?" squeaked Shelly. All her dreams of heroic magic fled before the reality now facing her.

"Yes," said Marcus. "You know how the spell works, and you have all of the documentation. It's up to you.

"The floors on that hall are supported by stone arches, so you should be safe for a while. But you don't have much time."

"Me? Alone?" asked Shelly. Fear filled her as the magnitude of the situation dawned on her. The castle, the town, and even her own life depended on her performing the spell correctly. Shelly put a hand against the wall to steady herself. The wall mushed inward at her touch.

"Yes," said Marcus. "Now go on. You don't have much time."

The reminder didn't help her nerves. Neither did the low creaking sounds that began to fill the hall.

"It's the weight of the eastern pigeon tower," Marcus noted. "You need to hurry."

After squeaking out another acknowledgement, Shelly turned and carefully returned to the room, conscious of each footstep on the stone floor.

The ingredients and tools lay on the table where she had

left them. She picked up the scroll and read the counterspell. It seemed simple enough. All she had to do was follow directions. With a deep breath, she set to work.

Fifteen minutes into the spell, Shelly encountered her first problem. The spell, while well designed and commented, called for a technique that she had never seen—the inverted triple wand loop.

"Inverted triple wand loop?" she asked aloud. The castle answered with a deep groan that sent a fresh spike of panic through her.

She briefly considered running back and finding Marcus, but she knew he wouldn't idly wait around in a collapsing castle. Either he had escaped to safety or he was searching for an alternate route up to her. Either way, she had no one to ask.

Looking around, Shelly spotted the spell's documentation: *Castle Repair Spell Manual v1.2.* She picked up the hundred-page supplement and flipped to the index. The inverted triple wand loop was on page 83.

There Shelly found detailed instructions for the inverted triple wand loop, including a series of stick figure illustrations. Although Marcus lacked all artistic skill, the wand motions were clear enough.

Holding the book open with her left hand, she performed the inverted triple wand loop. A flash of green light shot from the nearest bowl. She took that, and the lack of any catastrophic explosions, as a good sign.

Over the next three hours, Shelly worked through the entire spell. She returned to the documentation half a dozen times to look up important information. Each time, she found what she needed. The documentation even included a table of expected waiting times for different room temperatures, which took the guesswork out of determining when the third mixture was done.

Almost three and a half hours after she started, Shelly heard the familiar grinding of stone. The room's small window wobbled as the thin oval of glass transformed itself back into a neat circle.

Wispy clouds of dust floated through the air as rocks moved back into position. Outside the window, she heard a rising cheer.

She had succeeded.

Consistency

"I'M IMPRESSED," MARCUS SAID as Shelly climbed down the ladder that now led to the third floor. "The Castle Repair Spell was nontrivial. You did well."

"Thank you," Shelly managed. Casting the spell had drained her, and she could barely stand. She was vaguely aware of other people venturing into the castle to assess the damage.

As Shelly sank onto a small pile of rubble, the steward walked up to Marcus.

"It is fixed?" he asked.

Marcus sighed. "Yes. I told you it was fixed when we were outside. I told you it was fixed when we inspected the front gate. You can stop asking. It's fixed."

"You are certain?" asked the steward.

Marcus waved the steward away without responding. He turned to Shelly.

"Some people just don't trust magic," he said.

"Maybe his last experience with Hannaldous soured him on it," offered Shelly.

"Ha! Hannaldous is a hack."

Shelly tried to roll her eyes but didn't have the energy. "Uh-huh," she said.

"And how are you doing?" Marcus asked. "A spell like that can take a lot out of you. Wizards usually need to train for that type of spell."

"It was a lot harder than repelling bugs or silencing marching bands," Shelly agreed. "But I think I'm recovering."

"Good," said Marcus. He paused for a moment and looked off

into space. "I suppose this has been a good experience for you. The whole thing, I mean. Hannaldous's mistake, finding the counterspell, and even performing it. What a wonderful learning opportunity. I bet you see the value of a well-written spell and good documentation now."

Shelly nodded. "And the pain of a poorly written spell," she added.

"And comments?" asked Marcus.

"Good comments help," agreed Shelly.

She paused as she thought about her experience casting the spell. "The design, documentation, and comments all helped, but there was more," she said.

"What do you mean?" asked Marcus.

"The style helped," said Shelly. "You used the same style throughout the whole spell. Everything was consistent."

Shelly began to speak faster as the thoughts formed in her mind. The words began to gush out of her. "It's like the comment style you used, where every comment line is bright green, begins with '/*', and ends with '*/'. By the end of the spell I could easily distinguish the comments from the commands. It prevented at least two mistakes.

"Or how all the Boolean variables contained the word 'is' in their name, like IsDone or IsTimeToEatASnack. When I was performing the Spell of Moss Repellant, I was almost confused by the variable IsTime. If it hadn't been for the 'is,' I wouldn't have remembered it was a true or false value. I would have thought it stored a time variable."

"I suppose IsTime was a poor choice for a name," Marcus noted.

Shelly shrugged, "But your consistent style helped to make it clear."

Marcus smiled. "Another valuable lesson," he said. "Consistency improves understandability. You learn what to expect and how things are specified. You learn the naming conventions and what information you can find in comments. Above all else, consistency is key."

"Exactly," said Shelly. She pushed herself up from the pile of rubble and surveyed the hall. "Now that we've saved the castle, what's next?" she asked.

"A long backlog of potion orders and spell appointments," Marcus said. "I also have to create a new spell for the king. He needs something to prevent worms from giving away castle secrets. It'll be a challenging one."

"Can I help?" asked Shelly.

"If you remember the lessons of good design, then I would be happy to have your assistance."

"Not just collecting mold?" confirmed Shelly.

Marcus laughed. "Not just collecting mold," he agreed.

As Shelly packed up their equipment, she was filled with happiness. They had saved the castle, she had earned Marcus's trust, and there were new design challenges ahead.

Acknowledgements

A tremendous thanks goes out to all of the people who read earlier versions of this book and provided valuable feedback: Mike Hochberg, Edith Kubica, Regan Lee, Kristen Stubbs, and Phil Wagner. Thank you to Kristen Stubbs for suggesting the use of a picky patron for test-driven recipe development. Thank you to my editor, Marjorie Carlson, whose help was critical in vastly improving this work. Thank you to Meagan O'Brien for her wonderful cover design. A deep thank you to my family for their support.

About the Author

Jeremy Kubica began his career in computer science by learning to program a Commodore in the second grade. There he soon mastered the secret arts of variables and loops—skills that helped propel him toward fame and ever greater challenges.

He has a B.S. in Computer Science from Cornell University and a Ph.D. in Robotics from Carnegie Mellon University. He spent his graduate school years creating algorithms to detect killer asteroids (actually stopping them was, of course, left as 'Future work').

He is the author of *Computational Fairy Tales* and the Computational Fairy Tales blog.

Made in the USA
Charleston, SC
15 September 2015